A Small Book
of Short Stories

A D Small

ISBN-13: 9798454059477

Copyright © 2023 A D Small. All rights reserved.

The characters and events portrayed in this book are fictitious. Any similarity to real persons, living or dead, is coincidental and not intended by the author.

No part of this book may be reproduced, or stored in a retrieval system, or transmitted in any form or by any means, electronic, mechanical, photocopying, recording, or otherwise, without express written permission of the publisher.

Cover design by: Eagal Soul Ink

Contents

Shadow of the Beast	1
The Book	13
Entwined	23
37 Degrees	25
Depth	35
X Marks the Spot	61
The Cat	63
Face the Wall	67
Midnight Train	87
The Twitching Curtain	89
Blackout	101
Revelation	113
The First Book to Fall	115
The Audition	119
Acknowledgments	143
About A D Small	145
Books By A D Small	147

This book is dedicated to my Sweet Red, thank you for all the support with my writing and for pushing me to release my work. Also thank you to my mum for your full support and championing my work. A big thank you to all my friends and family who have given me support along the way.

And to the person reading the book now. I want to say thank you for taking the time to read it.

Shadow of the Beast

He clutched his chest and squinted as he ran through the sandstorm. His knees yearned to buckle. But the young man had to keep moving or be devoured by the savage beast. One which had stalked him for sixteen winters and left a trail of blood and death across the towns on the Northern Plains. His entire family had been slaughtered back when he had been a young boy. A howl pierced the night sky; and sent a sharp shiver down his spine. One word occupied his mind...RUN!

As he came over the ridge, he scanned the valley below. The moonlight caused something to glisten amongst the debris of a settlement. Hypnotised by the light he misplaced his feet and tumbled down the slope. He landed in a heap of pain and panic. His hands moved to his neck. Nothing. He had lost the amulet. Frantically he checked the slope. A few feet up the sand dune he saw a red glow. He scrambled to the group of rocks. Stuck in the cold coarse sand sat his amulet. He placed it over his head where it had been for the last sixteen winters.

Another howl echoed over the valley from beyond the ridge. He grasped the urgency to get some distance between himself and the savage beast. Even as his mind urged him to run, each step caused him immense pain. Across the settlement, stonewalls had submitted under the weight of the overgrown vines. They weaved through to the next building and the one after as if nature itself had attacked the settlement. But the vines had created holes, ones he could hide in, away from the beast.

He crawled through an opening in the third building. His heart still raced but as he slowed his breathing down, he began to retch. A foul stench came from the corner of the room. He shortened his gait as he cautiously passed through the shadows. Unaware of what lay in wake. Propped against the wall slumped a broken door. He lifted the wood and gasped in shear horror as he stared at the rotted corpse of a man, who sat in a puddle of dried blood. But his arms were wrapped tightly around a dirty blanket. With his hand over his mouth he pulled the blanket free, which revealed two more smaller decayed corpses. Both of them had their throats ripped out; their clothes stained

A Small Book

a dark red. He thought he could seek safety in the settlement for the night, so he could run again at daybreak.

The stench followed him as he moved around the room. He caught sight of piles of sticks and broken farming tools. In the farthest corner, a brisk breeze passed through a broken door with a symbol painted on it. Something the previous townsfolk used, a black circle with a red line going through it. He took a deep breath before he pushed the wood aside, behind it nothing but darkness. But as he stared into it the breeze passed through again, but a low crunch sound filled the silence like bones being broken. As the noise grew so did his fear. His mind told him to run but his body became heavy and cold. His eyes focused on the darkness, could it be the start of an incoming sandstorm or his mind playing tricks.

He saw something in the shadow and a low grumble came and slowly transformed into a growl. What appeared first from the shadows were two piercing blood red eyes. Ones with the intent to kill.

The beast entered into the room; dried blood dangled from its black matted fur around its jaw. Each snarl and growl revealed teeth jagged like the mountains of the Northern Ridge. As it edged closer to him, he stumbled backwards, and fell over a pile of rusted tools. Fear had its claws deep into him now. It

A D Small

advanced towards him; death had toxified the air. As if his hourglass of life had been broken and the sands drained away, becoming one with the dunes of the Northern Plain.

As he lay in amongst the sticks and tools. Something cold pressed against his skin. Blindly he fumbled around to find the end with a hope he could use it. Fear fought hard but with the possibility of a weapon, hope had the upper hand. With his eyes closed, he prayed to the gods for speed and strength. As he slowly raised his body the beasts gaze shifted to the amulet around his neck. He held hope in his hand in the form of a rusted shovel.

Every move he made the savage creature matched him, but it's gaze on the amulet never wavered. Round his neck hung the only thing he took from that horrific night. When the savage beast had massacred his family, making him an orphan. He edged back to the hole he came through, but he did not turn his back. As he blindly stepped through into the sandy streets his foot got caught in a twisted vine and he stumbled. But before he hit the floor the beast took a swing at him. Its claws dug trenches across his back, and he screamed with agony.

Under the moonlit sky in the space between two homes. He lay on his stomach as the bitter frigid air passed over him, but it brought with it a cloak of sand.

4

A Small Book

Which burned like the daytime beneath the planet's twin suns. But as the beast came through the hole in the wall. He had to make a choice, stand face to face with it or continue running for the rest of his life. But before he had the time to swing the shovel the beast had him pinned to the ground, the sand filled up the claw marks on his back. He looked up and focused his anger and rage at the predator which had stalked him.

"Do it, finish me off!"

Even as the saliva fell from the jaws of the beast hitting his cheek, he could hear its heart. It resembled the stampede from a herd of Great Auroch.

"Come on, do it, do it!!"

He turned his head as the beast sniffed and breathed down his ear. Made worse as it carried with it the stench of death. It moved to his chest and then it pawed at the amulet which resembled a half-moon. With one hand he snapped the string, which freed the amulet, and he slowly held it right in front of the beast. It snatched it from his hand and took a few steps back. His mind raced as he watched the beast paw the amulet. His decision would have an impact on his future, choose to reclaim the last reminiscence of his family or run for his freedom. The beast proceeded to howl at the moon. He watched it as it lowered its head and placed its paw on the amulet. Its jaw moved but no words or growls could be heard.

5

The sand screamed as he edged away slowly, which caused the beast's head to turn. As it moved towards him, he noticed its red eyes were now a light brown. It looked him up and down before it collapsed to the floor. Growls slowly turned to moans as it writhed around in pain. Its paws dug into the sand as its back arched and bones started to crack. Then it slammed into the ground and caused a sand cloud to rise around it. The thin veil of sand sparkled under the moonlight.

The beast's fur retracted and revealed weathered flesh. It howled as more bones cracked; its body slowly morphed into a man. He watched as the man raised his head to the sky before it looked at him. The mouth moved; again no words or sound came out. With dirt covered hands the man massaged his throat. Then it tried again.

"Son!"

The younger man fell to his knees, his eyes wide with bewilderment.

"Impossible! It can't be."

The younger man stared at the face before him. One he had not seen in over sixteen winters. One that had aged much like his, but the eyes hadn't changed, and more importantly he knew them. The man before him collapsed to his knees. He struggled back to his feet but collapsed again. But with each fall he tried

A Small Book

again, more determined than the last. After he mastered standing on two legs than his usual four, he attempted walking but his first few tries resembled a new-born Auroch. The young man watched his father stumble and reach out. A confused heart thumped loudly in his chest as he lunged forward and wrapped his cloak around his father. As he lowered him to the ground the young man went and gathered wood.

The flames crackled; he looked through them towards his father who had a firm grip on the amulet.

The flames caused the amulet to glisten, as the young man drifted back to the horrific night.

Woken in the night by his mother and father arguing. His older brother perched on the edge of the bed turned and pressed a finger against his lips. They sat and listened; words were muffled but then screams of agony followed. His brother ran for the door.

"Stay? No matter what you hear."

Fear of being alone in the darkness caused him to follow his brother into the hallway. They edged towards their parents' bedroom door as more screams filled the air. His brother reached for the handle, but then the door flew open and knocked him through the air. As his brother hit the wall, he heard a crack as his body slumped to the floor. He ran to his brother and watched his eyes drain of life, and his chest fall for the last time.

"Mother! Father!!"

But no response came. As he approached the shattered doorway, he peered inside. His mother's broken body lay against the foot of the bed. Her neck torn open, and fresh blood soaked into the wooden slats of the floor. He saw her eyes as they rolled into the back of her head. The beast stepped into the doorway and blocked his path. It growled with rage filled eyes, focused on the only person left in the house alive. As the young child curled up in fear the beast stopped, growled, and then ran out of the house.

When he woke, he saw something glisten in his mother's dead hand. His father's amulet. For years he had wondered why his dad could not be found, why hadn't he protected his family. A mystery which had now been solved.

"I hoped I could find a cure but nothing and no one throughout the Northern Plains could help. I am sorry you have had to live on the run and carry the pain alone."

"How did this all start? I can see the bite mark on your shoulder."

"I was a similar age to your brother, out on a hunting trip in the west valleys with my father. Our

A Small Book

camp came under attack from a pack of Graycanis. During the attack, one of them bit me. I was close to death when my father returned and saved me. He then gave me the amulet as a gift for my protection. Similar to what he had around his neck."

One question overshadowed the explanation his father had given on why he turned into the beast.

"You killed mother?" he cried.

"I... I am sorry my son. I am sorry about your brother too. It will haunt me for the rest of my days."

"Why?!" he said angrily.

"The Rage takes over you. The urge is strongest when the moon is fullest. The amulet held the beast and thirst at bay."

"Learn to control it! Fight it, you must!"

"I don't think I can. I can feel it my veins. The rage is too strong."

As he stared at his father with a conflicted heart. He began to wonder if his father could control the rage now, he is reunited with his amulet. The young man rose and took a deep breath before a tear rolled down his cheek. From the fire he grabbed a piece of wood and caught his father squarely in the jaw. In a small bush he found a rusted shovel. He managed to cut some of the vine which hung from the side of the building. The young man paused before he snatched the amulet from his father's bound hands.

As the flames grew the young man's vision fixated on the amulet as he turned it over in his hand. A groan from his father broke his hypnotic state.

"Give it to me!"

The young man could see the rage in his fathers' eyes. Could the curse be creating this anger or feeding what is already there. He looked deep inside himself and pondered if he had the same rage.

"Give it to me now!!"

The silver moon glistened as it crept through the clouds. He watched as his father fought the binds. As if the light of the moon brought forth waves of anger. His father's eyes locked on to his, then the transformation started. Light brown eyes turned to a savage red; the fangs sprang free. His head looked up to the sky and let out a blood curdling howl which echoed through the settlement. His bones cracked as they morphed into the beast. Then the binds snapped, and he collapsed on all fours. Its backed arched and cracked as it readjusted. As he writhed in agony, his weathered skin sprouted fur.

Sadness clogged the young man's mind as he bore witness to the transformation. Run, the only word which shone brighter than any other. But he had been running his entire life and he wanted to stop, he

A Small Book

wanted a life and his own family. With what he now knew, he had to fight. The beast circled the fire slowly, with each step it growled and frothed at the mouth. Without taking his focus off the creature he seized another piece of wood from the fire and swung wildly in its direction. He froze as it coiled backwards and leapt towards him. The young man swung and missed which allowed the beast it to sink its jaw around his shoulder. As warm blood dripped down his back. He screamed in pain and collapsed to the floor. Blood dripped from the mouth of the beast as it growled at the young man. Unable to move his arm above his head he swapped the wood to his weaker arm and rose to his feet.

"I am too tired to run. So do it! Come on, do it!!"

As the beast leapt forward the young man swung the wood as hard as he could. He heard a crunch as they collided and before landing in a heap on the floor. As he looked down, he saw a piece of wood protruding from the creature's chest. Blood soaked into the terrain as the beast's breath slowed

down and stopped. The young man grimaced as he tried to get to his feet. He staggered over to the beast, fear crept into his mind. His foot caught something lay on the ground. Without breaking the gaze on the beast's prone body, he fumbled around, and grabbed a piece of wood attached to some rough cold metal. His

11

father still hadn't moved so he glanced down at his hand. Another tear rolled down his face as he raised the shovel above his head. He brought it down with all the force he could muster. The head rolled and blood soaked the ground around it. With the stained shovel in his hand he slowly dug his father's grave. He placed the head and the body into the hole, pain coursed through his body as he covered the grave with rocks. With a strip torn from his cloak he placed his arm in a sling. He used his uninjured arm and placed the amulet around his neck. As he sat and stared up at the night sky, his shoulder began to burn.

The Book

Written in an old vintage font, the words 'Never-Ending Books' sat in the middle of a slightly weather worn custom built sign. Which sat above a glass window covered in layers of dirty fingerprints. The shops on either side had their shutters closed, small alarm boxes flashed intermittently. A faint light moved towards the shop front from the inside, the light increased and slowly engulfed the window. Crash. Each piece of glass sang down the street before they hit the floor. Then a thud as a hooded figure landed on the ground with one arm over his eyes, the other tightly held a book against his chest. Glass crunched under foot as he sprinted down the street.

The picture of his wife Emma and his son Michael tied up ran through his head. As he made his way towards the east side of town. Steps one and two done on the checklist. The third step get the book to Ms Shaw at Queensbridge Station. Sounds of crunched glass caused him to glance over his shoulder. Three men dressed in dark grey suits appeared from the broken shop window of 'Never-Ending Books'. No sign of lights or movement from inside any of the nearby buildings. Everyone seemed to be asleep, unaware of the chase which unfolded in the streets. As he came to the junction he headed right to the town square, every route to the east of town branched off from there. He had no idea who the men in suits worked for, but he didn't want to get close enough to ask. Follow the instructions and his wife and son would be safe. The mysterious Ms Shaw told him the task when she appeared in his life over a week ago and flipped his world upside down. With the book tightly gripped in his arms he ran.

He had no idea he would be hunted by these men in suits. But they had appeared not long after he had stolen the book from Arthur Robbins the owner of the book shop. An experienced thief he had been for fifteen years but an Olympic athlete he had not been. Questions sprung into his head with every beat of his heart. What made this book important? Why did Ms Shaw need it so much? Who were the men pursuing him? Why did he have to steal it? His legs burned with every step, but he had to run, his family needed him.

A Small Book

He pulled the book close to his chest and headed left at the next junction. A car turned on to the street in front of him; people climbed out and walked to a door at the side of a shop. He recognised one guy as a security guard from his works, he tried to recall his name as he slowly walked over to him.

"Hey, Brian!"

But his work colleague did not recognise him as they passed each other, no acknowledgement from Brian or any of the group. What is going on, David thought, as he rushed down the street. At the next junction he took glanced at the signposts, he took the right towards the church. Not even the breeze of the night wind could cool him down.

He burst through the beam of light which covered the entrance of the courtyard. Frantically he tried the handles of the three doors down the side of the church, but none would open. His lungs clawed for air, but his mind pushed him to keep moving. As car brakes screeched beyond the sacred ground, his heartbeat raced. He looked towards the far corner beyond the Livingstone catacomb and identified the moss-covered part of the wall. Muffled voices closely followed by footsteps entered the courtyard. The hairs on David's neck stood up, as a loud hum reverberated around the sacred ground; each pulse caused the tombstones to tremble. Then pop, followed by a bright aniline light engulfed every inch of the ground. Another half a dozen tombstones exploded. As the rubble rained down, David darted for the wall. More bursts of light fought against the white floodlights of the church. He squeezed through one of the holes, but his jacket snagged on some wire mesh which protruded from the broken wall. As another hum started, David fought against the wave of panic as he attempted to free himself. Images of his wife and child flashed in his mind but disappeared once a purple light engulfed him. Another blast sent David and the wall across the grass verge towards the canal.

As the ground tremored around him, he lay there and gazed up at the aniline light show in the sky. He tried to stand but his bodies broken equilibrium caused him to stumble through the rubble. Anxiety and fear set in when he realised, he no longer had the book. Muffled voices became clearer as he scanned the demolished wall. He spotted the piece of his jacket caught between chunks of debris, which had created a makeshift stone tepee. Below it sat the book bound in a leather cover and a strap which had kept the pages safe. He pulled it to his chest and scaled up the embankment to the bridge.

An aniline blast sent a cloud of dirt and shredded grass into the air. With his raised arm he shielded his eyes as he made his way over the bridge towards the

A Small Book

station. Another bolt of energy shook the ground underfoot. On the other side, he could hear the voice come through the tannoy system.

"The southbound train to Kings Gate will arrive at the station in 5 minutes. Please make your way to the platform ready for boarding and mind the gap."

He reached inside his jacket pocket, but all his fingers found were the frayed edges of the hole. His head sank along with his spirit, the train ticket lost in the pursuit, but he had the book. The path and the signpost led David to platform four. His lungs fought for air, as his calf muscles tightened, the numbness moved up to his knees. But he ignored the pain and thought of Emma and Michael being held hostage. Voices came from the church wall, but he didn't want to turn around, so he just ran through the unguarded gate and onto the platform.

As he moved through the crowd, he spotted the train down the track. A woman in a black jacket and pants scowled as she inspected David before she turned around and headed out of the station along with the others. As he watched this; other people started to leave. He stood in front of a young man who wore the station uniform, but he just barged past David without an apology. More people left, a young woman abandoned her suitcase and a pram by a bench. As each one passed him, he saw their vacant faces. Then he noticed two suited men as they fought against the tide of the crowd, each of them held a large metal gauntlet. Both had an aniline glow, and a humming sound rang around the platform.

He gripped the book tighter and closed his eyes. His ripped jacket flapped in the breeze as the train pulled in and screeched to a halt. Before the doors opened, he caught his reflection in the glass and his stomach churned. He could see a grey streak had formed in his caramel matted hair; but the redness in his eyes looked sore. The job for Ms Shaw had been completed, now she had to release Emma and Michael. Then they could go home and put this nightmare behind them all.

"Get on board now," she said firmly.

As he boarded the train, he saw the dark blonde hair of Ms Shaw as she stood with her back to David. But then she started to speak in a foreign tongue and at the same time a red glow emanated from her leather gloved hands. Within moments it engulfed the whole carriage which they all occupied. Aniline blasts bounced off the carriage, but no harm befell any of them. As he looked to Ms Shaw's left, he saw Emma, her eyes red from the tears which rolled down her face. She ran her hands through Michael's auburn hair. As the train pulled away from the station, he stepped towards them both.

"Did they hurt you, babe? How is Michael?" he said.

As he wrapped his arms around her waist and pulled her in tight. She burrowed her head into his chest.

"I'm OK, love. Michael is sleeping. Did you get the book?" she said eagerly.

"Yes, here it is!" he said.

He held the book outstretched, eager to complete the trade. With her gloved hands Ms Shaw stepped forward and took it. She held it aloft and smiled, then placed it in a satchel. A humming sound whirred behind him. As he turned around the face of his wife disappeared and revealed the face of another woman.

"What are you doing? What have they done to you?" he said with a tremor.

A woman with silver streaks in her brown hair now pointed her spinning metal gauntlet at him. He frantically looked around the carriage. With an outstretched arm Ms Shaw pointed at the chair behind David. His wife and son lay motionless.

"Ms Shaw, we made a deal. Steal the book and you would return my wife and son to me."

She turned, removed the dark shades; her jade-coloured eyes stared directly at David. They glistened under the neon lights on the train.

"Have I not returned them to you."

As rage took control, he lunged forward but then froze, as an unseen force gripped him. The woman with silver streaks moved forward with her gauntlet held up towards David. The tannoy clicked into life.

"Next stop will be Wickford. May we remind all passengers to mind the gap when exiting the train. We would also like to remind all passengers, if you see anything suspicious, please speak to staff or the British Transport Police Immediately,"

He then noticed Ms Shaw grab the satchel and headed for the door as it pulled into the next station. She turned and looked at David with those eyes of jade.

"You will start to feel the burning, in your lungs first and then your head before the rest of your body. I won't' lie this will hurt immensely. But we of the Hell Shadow deeply appreciate what you have done for us."

As the train halted, he saw the empty dimly lit platform. The doors opened and Ms Shaw stepped into the shadows. The woman who remained turned her wrist and David moved to face Emma and Michael. He fought to turn away, but the two bodies lay against the carriage wall, both of them with faces contorted and frozen in fear. Tears rolled down his face as he moved closer. Blood had seeped from their eyes and patches of their skin had turned black.

The woman with silver streaks in her hair turned

him around to face her; he saw her black doll like eyes, void of life. But a wicked smile painted another picture. As she rotated her wrist David unleashed a guttural scream as his arms and legs unnaturally contorted and snapped. As she clenched her fist, his ribs cracked. Then his chest tightened, and he struggled to breathe. As he hit the floor, she held the gauntlet over his head and uttered some words. She then stepped off the train and into the darkness. As he lay there his head began to burn from the inside. He tried to reach for his wife, but death had arrived, and he slipped into his own darkness.

Entwined

I curl next to her and stroke her face like I used to. She shivers and sinks deeper into the duvet. At the same time, every night she opens her eyes and looks to her right, but I'm not there. Her eyes well up, as I whisper.

"Same time tomorrow."

37 Degrees

His hand glided over the keypad as he entered the keycode. The seal broke on the only entry and exit of the room, it hissed and popped open. As he heaved the thick metal door open, Austin heard a clunk outside the farming room. He looked up and down the surgical white panelled corridor, but he couldn't see or hear anything.

"Hank, is that you?" he called out.

No response came, so he stepped inside. The digital gauge read Thirty-nine degrees, two degrees more than the ideal room temperature. But Austin hadn't noticed the green light above the door turn red, just for a moment, before he closed the door. The warning indicated the room temperature had peaked forty degrees.

He had been at Soul Farm Eight for just over two

years, Austin knew he had to put in the hours and exceed the quota of souls set by the head of the farming facility, all this would help him gain the promotion. The next submission meeting would be in three months. He had met all the quotas set by his supervisor, Hank Walters. So he hung all his hope on the promotion, as it would mean a move to another farm. This would be his last quarter to up his quota before he stood in front of the panel. He tolerated Hank's superiority complex, as he knew; one day he would surpass him and have the opportunity to put him in his place.

The steel walkway clanged under Austin's footsteps as he approached the computer terminal. He placed his security card into the slot on his keyboard and entered his password. In pride of place above the monitor hung a hand carved photo frame. It held a picture of himself, his beloved wife Catherine and son Charlie, their last holiday before she passed away. He remembered the day well, the sun shone bright, and the cool breeze had blown her auburn hair across her face, but her eyes were a piercing emerald, green. Every time he looked at the picture; it caused him to freak out as her eyes stared directly into his aching soul. His eyes then fell to the picture of little Charlie who had curly blonde hair, but he had gained his mother's dimples as well as her eyes.

Footage of the soul fields filled the screen and then slowly cycled through all fourteen cameras placed around the room. On another screen, Austin looked at the room's temperature readings, but worry kicked in as he noticed the spike in temperature when he had entered the room. His eyes scanned each screen, nothing seemed out of the ordinary. The current batch of souls held in this room, each weighed twenty-one grams. But as he got to soul eighty-eight, he noticed it weighed eight grams less.

He left his post and stood at the steel rails. His gaze fell across the field, it had a soft blue glow which flowed like the ocean tides. The souls at farm eight were to be sold to the masses by the company ReSoul. He wondered what it would be like to implant a second soul inside his body. News stations reported the positive side of housing two souls in one body, how it aged people slowly, improved health and strength. But a few years after the first soul farms were built, rumours of the Soul Jackers started to spread. Nobody knows where the first one came from but when they appeared things began to change. The first soul bank robbery happened. All the large soul companies put a stop to the negative reports, as investors didn't want anything to affect the profit margin. When Austin first started, he questioned the staff about the negative reports, but he soon learned to keep his mouth shut.

He picked up his key and activated the eighth panel on the soul field. As he moved along the walkway, the platform began to rise from the field. Each soul sat inside a see-through plastic cube, Austin saw the broken one, its flame glowed like a burnt amber not the bright cyan like the others. A metal crane arm unfolded from the ceiling, it lowered itself, he heard a click and watched the section of the field rise up to the same level as the rails of the walkway. The crane arm moved the souls towards the inspection bay. It tilted slightly as Austin approached it; he placed his hands on the pair of gloves on the bench. Each pair were made from a finely woven Tanium alloy, created by Dr Tsung as a precautionary measure. As the first person who ever touched a soul had burn marks on his hands, scientists, doctors and the media named it, Soul Burn.

He reached for the broken soul housed in plastic cube which gently held with two hands, Austin's eyes transfixed on the flickering flame. Carefully he clicked it into the inspection pod and observed a small metal ring covered in lights, move up and down. It did it four times slowly before it stopped, a small ruby coloured light shone brightly. He then picked up the cube and cautiously walked over to the Soul Containment Unit. The cylinder-shaped machine filled the corner of the room from ceiling to floor, it had a small door in the middle, as he moved closer it opened automatically.

A Small Book

He placed the cube inside the slot and waited for the red light to turn green, so he could hit the switch and watch the cube disappear in the flames of the furnace. As he reached for the switch; shattered glass echoed around the farm.

"Hank?" he mused,

No response came as he moved back towards the computer terminal. On the floor lay the broken photo frame, the crack in the glass ran between Austin and Charlie. The words on the computer screen changed and Austin's calmness transformed into blind panic. He checked his pockets but, he couldn't find the security card. He dropped to his knees and checked under the terminal. Ouch. As he inspected his hand, blood trickled down his palm from the small shard of glass imbedded in his skin. He placed the broken photo on the terminal, his hand hovered over the alarm button. Fear of being demoted or worse entered his mind. His hands rifled through his pockets again as he walked back to the inspection bay, still no security pass.

As he stood in the inspection bay, he noticed all the souls on the raised section began to move in the same direction. Again Austin checked his pocket and picked up the gloves. Then panic turned to fear as he noticed the door of the soul containment unit had been opened, and the burnt amber coloured soul had vanished. His heart raced and everything became blurred as he spun around on his heels. The blue flames snapped him back into focus, as he ran to them, he noticed they were now standing tall. But as he looked across the soul farm, he could see the flames further up the field lean towards the walkway then back to their normal positions. As the field flowed, his fear turned into dread, and he ran for the alarm button. He had sprinted about ten metres when something slammed him against the metal rails.

He writhed in pain and clutched his lower back. A shimmer passed by him as he ran his hand over his head; shocked as he saw his hand covered in blood. Dizziness and pain kicked in. The shimmer moved towards him, Austin panicked and scurried backwards, but it followed. Fear caused his muscles to freeze, he closed his eyes and repeated.

"This can't be real."

Then the shimmer slammed Austin into the wall with force. Its grip tightened around his throat, his lungs fought, and his vision blurred. Then he slipped into unconsciousness.

As he came around, he found himself lay on the floor in a heap. He looked around, the shimmer had gone. He struggled to stand but pushed himself to move towards the computer terminal. As Austin passed the soul field, something hit him, and he collapsed onto the guard rail. His lungs emptied and

A Small Book

he heard a crack, with every breath the pain pinned Austin down to the walkway. He reached out with his hand as he saw the photograph of Catherine fall from the wall, but it slipped through his fingers. He closed his eyes and heard the glass break. The pain pinned him down, every breath repeatedly pierced his lungs. Pain and fear pinned him to the floor as the shimmer approached; it slowly tilted its head to the side. Intermittently the shimmer flickered and began to change in front of Austin. It revealed a man dressed all in black, with a long-hooded jacket. His gloved hand pressed a button on a small device that hung from his jacket. Then Austin began to hear the heavy breathing of the hooded man. A dry raspy voice spoke clearly.

"I see you."

The figure dropped his hood. For only a moment Austin caught the fear trapped in his own eyes. As his face reflected off the black panels in the goggles. The mans gloved hands removed the mask to reveal a bald scarred head, who's eyes were dark emerald. No images had been disclosed by ReSoul or the News reports. But he knew the man had to be a Soul Jacker.

The hooded man removed the broken soul he had taken from the containment unit and held it over Austin. They both watched the amber flame as it dimmed and flickered. Then the eyes of the Jacker locked onto his, Austin sat mesmerised by the emerald eyes.

Something cold pierced Austin's skin and snapped him from his trance. As he writhed in pain he caught sight of the soul, he watched it change to a dark angry red. He screamed, as a pain twisted and contorted his stomach. The soul jacker then pulled some metallic objects from his jacket and placed them on the table. The dread of death crept over him, as he heard pieces being clicked together. Shards of glass sliced Austin's hands as he crawled away from the Soul Jacker. When the device had been placed on his chest his muscles began to contract. But as he lay prone on the floor, he could see the bright lights swing overhead. The dark shadow could be seen before he heard the glass break. A gloved hand came down and held his head, then a voice spoke.

"The soul is an amazing thing, each one should be and is different, unique. But these farms create uniformed souls, generic. For what a quick fix, a high or is it for the control and the money. Taking away free will, by controlling the drug which everybody now craves."

The Soul Jacker clipped a device over Austin's face, fear took over. His pupils widened when a pair of goggles covered his eyes. Nothing but darkness

A Small Book

followed by pain, as the Soul Jacker forced Austin's jaw open to place in a mouthguard. Keep your eyes closed, Austin thought.

"I won't lie, this will sting, but it will hurt a lot more if you fight it."

With his eyes shut, Austin listened, he heard a beep before an electric pulse shot through his head. He tried to resist but the pulse became more frequent, he could see the bright light breaking the darkness. Another burst of pain came, and he could no longer fight, he opened his eyes to the light. Then the heat came, beads of sweat escapes every pore on his face. But the worst pain ever came from his chest, which moved into his head, then to his eyes, as if something had reached deep inside him. Then complete darkness.

As he came to, the metal grates of the walkway began to move underneath Austin, but no fear came, just a void. As the mask left his face the lights which hung from the ceiling didn't seem bright like they were before. Gloved hands unclipped the device from Austin's chest, and he could see the faint blue light which came from inside the jacket of the Soul Jacker.

"By the time you can move again, I will be long gone."

With an emptiness which anchored Austin to the

floor, he watched on as the Soul Jacker pressed something on his wrist, lifted his hood over his head, and disappeared.

Depth

"Drain the catching bay, Ari," Captain Ferris Ferrago demanded, verbally guiding his crew from his commander's seat on the deck of the Dee-Alma - a merchant vessel he'd won in a game of Raanga Roulette.

"Aye, Captain," Ari replied, acknowledging the legendary commander.

With his one functioning eye, Ferrago overlooked the catching bay on the main monitor. The large metal net held his catch in place against the corrugated bay floor. As the sea water drained away, the gargantuan sea monster became visible. Despite clearly writhing in discomfort, it made no sound. Noting his findings for future study and reference, he found the creature to be extremely odd. Zooming in closer, he awed at its appearance - worm-like and covered in independently moving nodules, he accurately guessed it's length to be thirty feet. Crossing the balcony with his line of sight firmly on the sea creature's head, Ferrago couldn't help but marvel at its powerful, snapping jaw lined with razor sharp, almost metallic-looking teeth.

"Cerso, prep it for cryogenic stasis. I want to be back on Tellus Six before Earth Day," Ferrago admitted; he'd never had any love for the Tartica system or for all-water based planets loaded with extreme danger; however, he did enjoy fruitful bounties and rich paydays, and so did his specially selected, hand-picked crew.

"Aye, Captain."

Bringing his right hand up to his breast plate, Ferrago activated the ship's comms. With the simple touch of his thumb against a touch-sensitive pad, he addressed his men over the ship's tannoy. "Each of you, you're here for your own reasons," he began. "Money, to escape, or for the adventure. Whatever those reasons are, you've served this mission well. We've caught the beast and earned our payday. Our employers will be incredibly pleased with this catch - they'll reward us handsomely for it. So, let us prepare for our journey to Tellus Six. In two days, we'll be singing and dancing, and fucking."

Rudely interrupting Ferrago's message to his crew before he could bring it to the usual rousing conclu-

A Small Book

sion, the ship's siren sounded. Pulsating amber, the alarm beacons lit up the catching bay. "Everyone, to your stations. Now," Ferrago growled.

Dashing to their respective workstations, the crew followed the ship's safety protocols, to the letter, clipping themselves securely in their seats using the built in seat belts and harnesses.

Taking his seat on the deck, Ferrago pressed his number one and right-hand man for information, "What was that, Driff? I don't see it on the radar."

"I don't know, Captain. It came from the deep. Nothing. Then, it was just there. It's out there. Somewhere."

"I need an exact location. Somewhere isn't enough. I want eyes on it now. Bring up the live feed on the main screen, Driff. All external cameras."

Staring at the main screen, Ferrago pressed a thumb against his breast plate again, using the touch-sensitive pad to bring alive his augmented cybernetic eye piece, allowing him to see the finest details onscreen. "Check the port side, Driff. Eight hundred meters," he demanded, exuding absolute respect and control.

"Aye, Captain."

Filled with anticipation, Driff and the rest of the deck crew watched on as a red dot moved ominously close to the ship, on the radar. Unworried, Ferrago

37

allowed a wry smile to creep across his pale face; he'd lived his whole adult life chasing prey to order. Plus, he knew his ship well - the Dee-Alma had survived much worse, he confidently told himself, and she'd survive worst to come.

Closing in on the ship, thick and fast, the red dot would soon hit them. Using his unrivalled experience, Ferrago estimated it'd be bigger than the sea creature frozen in the cryogenic unit. "Driff, I want you to put some room between us and that thing. I want it to chase us, then we circle back and drop anchor. Let's see if we can't double our payload, shall we?"

"Aye, Captain," Driff nodded.

Fully utilising his own unique skill set and the ship's powerful thrusters, Driff pushed the Dee-Alma harder.

Standing to his feet, Ferrago sprinted towards the ship's stern, desperate to see the threat himself, through his good eye and his augmented cybernetic eye piece. Arriving at the stern, he stared out of the rear porthole and saw another sea worm. Much like the worm on ice in the cryo unit, its jaw chomped furiously.

Activating his comms again, Ferrago reached out to Ari. "How's our guest in the cryo unit getting on, Ari?"

"All good, Captain."

A Small Book

"Prepare the neighbouring chamber, we'll soon be doubling our catch."

Returning to his seat of command, Ferrago saw another two dots appear on the radar screen, then a third. Glancing across the waterline, he couldn't see anything on the port or starboard sides. Another dot appeared then they all strangely disappeared. "I'll be in the catching bay if I'm needed, Driff," Ferrago told him. "You have the command."

"Aye, Captain."

The first catch of the day writhed in frustration in the catching bay. Staring hard, Ferrago again noted the creature's mouth. Curiously studying it, he could physically see the agitated anger in its every movement. Releasing no sound to accompany its struggle for freedom, it continued to thrash and throw its considerable weight at its restraints.

Moving away from the head, he turned his attention to the tail end, which hung loosely out of the net. Quivering and jerking, the tail opened and secreted a strange cobalt-blue liquid. Oozing outwards, the goo ran down the ship's steel drainage grids.

As the ship shook, Ferrago watched on as Ritti fell over the balcony and hit the catching bay floor hard. Instinctively, he rushed to Ritti's aid.

Emitting more blue liquid and a new, foul stench,

the worm prompted Ritti to gag and vomit, spilling his lunch in chunks.

"Move it, Ritti," Ferrago growled, as precious time ticked away. "There's no time for a weak belly."

Steadying himself, Ritti wiped the sick from his mouth. Stepping backwards, he slipped on the blue goo and fell, painfully hitting the cast iron floor again. Attempting to stand, he saw something in the liquid stir and move towards him. "Captain, what the hell is that?"

Before Ferrago could respond, Ritti screamed out in pain, collapsing to the floor, doubled over in the most intense pain he'd ever experienced. Upon closer inspection, Ferrago saw something horrific - a smaller version of the giant worm had burrowed into the gut of his trusted crew member. Spilling short, sharp, spurts of blood from his mouth, Ritti let out a dying, blood-curdling scream and fell silent. Rolling Ritti over onto his back, Ferrago reeled in horror when he saw the deep purple-coloured blood on his crew member's uniform and around his lips. Stepping back, the captain's chest plate lit up to the voice of Driff over the comms. "Captain, we have a big problem," he yelled above the busy, background noise.

"Copy. We have one here, too," Ferrago told Driff. "Thirty foot, and Ritti's dead."

A Small Book

"Shit,' Driff cursed. "I liked Ritti."

Neither Ferrago or Driff spoke for a second or two, despite the urgency for words and a desperate need for a plan of defence. Taking control, Ferrago wanted to understand the secondary danger they faced. "What's going on with you, son? What's the situation?"

"We've got three fifty footers closing in on us, Captain. If we don't do something, we're done for."

"Until the hull is compromised beyond repair, the threat down here is more important. I'll get to you soon."

"Aye, Captain."

"In the meantime, try not to shit yourself, OK?" Ferrago laughed.

Driff smiled to himself, safe in the knowledge he had no immediate plans to soil his underwear.

Darting towards the catching bay control room, sprinting as fast as his legs could carry him, Ferrago arrived at the main operating computer terminal. "Ari, move. I need your seat."

"Captain," Ari nodded, vacating his seat without question; Ferrago held his absolute respect because he'd proven himself a great captain, who'd never once failed a crew under his command.

Navigating the ship's operational systems like only he could, Ferrago hit the console switches and lowered the rods and the metal net. Tapping the comms button on his chest plate, he reached out to his first officer, desperate for more information so he could attack the situation in the best way. "How close is the worm, Driff?"

"Four hundred meters and closing, Captain," Driff worryingly replied, the fear had become palpable in his voice.

Charging the ship's electric capture rods, Ferrago lowered them into the water. He began the countdown with the hope of capturing the worm in the hull. "Five...four...three... two...one!"

The crew watched as the electricity cut through the water between the rods, which didn't at all affect the giant worm. Instead, it repeatedly crashed itself into the iron walls of the hull, using its heavy mass to devastating effect.

"Captain, more threats are nearing," Driff advised his leader, his eyes fixed on the radar monitor. "The hull shield is in danger of being further compromised; we won't survive them all. Permission to take off?"

"Driff, make it so," Ferrago nodded, getting to work at fighting back against the furious and hungry worm smashing apart the walls in the lower part of the ship. Retracting the rods, he winched in the net, as the ship pulled out of the water. Holding onto his seat as the ship tipped to the port side, Ari gulped.

A Small Book

Standing to his feet, Ferrago shifted swiftly towards the stairwell near the balcony to assess the situation from a different viewpoint. Before he could think, another heavy hit from the worm shook the ship, tipping it towards the starboard side. Falling backwards, over the rails, he hit the catching bay floor with a heavy crunch.

Winded, Ferrago struggled to stand, but did so through sheer will. Discombobulated from his fall, he staggered towards Ritti's dead body despite the pain searing through him. Nearing the corpse, he could taste the acidic, blue liquid from the worm in the air. Gagging, he managed to hold the vomit back. Looking down at Ritti, his dead eyes were glass-like.

Without warning, another worm crawled from Ritti's stomach. Horrified, Ferrago knew the severity of his situation - the longer he remained in catching bay with the worms, the slimmer his chances were of surviving. Grabbing the chain hanging from the balcony, he put the agony tearing through him to one side and began to desperately climb.

Whipping at him with its tail, the giant worm hit him on the side of his non-functioning eye, knocking him to the floor, further amplifying his physical pain and growing fear.

Dazed, Ferrago's whole world began to spin. Struggling to focus, he made every effort to escape but, before he could get to his knees, the smaller worm aggressively attached itself to his bicep. Ripping open his flesh, the worm tightened its grip on his arm - the more he struggled, the more pressure it applied. Screaming out in distress, his humerus shattered, yet the worm remained attached to his now nearly-dead limb, completely restricting the blood flow to his forearm and hand.

Near to passing out, Ferrago's saw his enemy - the sea worm connected to his upper arm - had now quickly doubled in size. Making a last-ditch effort to live, he reached for the chain again. Mere inches away from grabbing hold of it, the ship tipped again. Collapsing onto the body of Ritti, Ferrago noticed a change in the worm - it'd formed nodules, which began to cut through his deadened, mangled arm, severing it completely. For the remaining time he had left, he'd forever remember the disturbing sound as his arm hit the floor.

As if from nowhere, another smaller worm appeared behind the contained giant worm. Hungrily feasting on the blood from Ferrago's deadened limb, it promptly doubled in size. Staggering wearily backward, the punch-drunk captain slipped on the goo again and hit the floor with a heavy crunch. Confused and scared like never before, though you'd never have known it, he neared unconsciousness. Slipping into a

A Small Book

pool of coldness, everything around him suddenly darkened.

Then, from the darkening abyss, a familiar voice cut through the silence to pull him back. "Captain, stay with us, we're on our way to you. Focus on my voice. Captain? Can you hear me?" Ari called out.

Arriving at Ferrago's location the look of horror swept Ari's face. Taking a moment to inspect Ferrago's mangled arm and bloody stump, he saw first-hand the exponential growth of the baby worm, as it continued to feast. Determined to stop its threat to the Dee-Alma and crew, he swung a metal harpoon in its direction, giving Dr Lukman the ship's chief medical officer, the necessary time to inject a needle into Ferrago's torn flesh. As the quick-acting drugs flowed through Ferrago's body, he felt his pain abate; within a second the pain had almost subsided and his mind instantly became clearer.

"The other worms are pulling us down, Captain. We can't take much more. We need to do something," Ari advised Ferrago, hopeful his captain could formulate a plan of action to save them all.

"I have an idea," Ferrago replied with staggered breath.

"I always knew you would, Captain. What do we do?"

"Contain the smaller worms."

"How?"

"Any way you can."

"What about the big one?"

"We flush it. That'll buy us the time we need. In the meantime, get me to the medical bay. I need patching up."

"Aye, Captain."

Fitting Ferrago with a shoulder-and-waist harness, Ari clipped him to the chain. Hoisting Ferrago upwards and away from the danger, the crew on the upper level pulled him to safety and quickly rushed him to the medical bay.

Working well together, Ari and Cerso used their own personal stun guns to incapacitate the three baby worms, ahead of transferring them to the cryogenic laboratory for stasis. The giant worm, still bound in the catching bay net, continued to throw its weight against the metal walls. Frustrated and upset its spawn had been snatched away, it opened its mouth and screamed in a terrifying silence.

Alone in the catching bay with only the deceased Ritti for company, the giant worm's anger kept it going relentlessly strong. Watching it wildly thrash from the med bay monitor, Ferrago knew they had just one shot to save themselves. Dependant on perfect timing, he prayed his risky gamble would pay off. A gambling man by nature, he'd always take the risk. From his bed

A Small Book

in the medical bay, Ferrago activated his comms via his chest plate. "Driff?"

"I'm here, Captain. Awaiting further instruction."

"Ari and Cerso, are they with you? Are they safe?" Ferrago asked, worried for two of his most trusted and capable crew members.

"Aye, all present and accounted for, Captain. Cerso has deep cut to his arm, but he says he's good."

"The infant worms? Where are they?"

"On ice, Captain."

"Good. Driff, hit full speed and release the worm from the net."

"But, Captain," Driff fearfully stammered, terrified that by releasing the worm, it'd make a move over the top-level balcony and attack the deck.

Securing himself to his bed using the attached safety straps, Ferrago had no time for being afraid. "Driff, that's a direct order, son. Now's not the time to be scared. I picked you to be my number one for a reason. Now, get your shit together."

"But, Captain,' Driff stammered again.

"Trust me, this is MY ship, I know what she can do, and I know what YOU can do."

As commanded, Driff used the ship's controls to release the worm. As expected, it raised its ugly head and aggressively lurched upwards.

A D Small

"Drop the rear anchors, I want the ship's nose pointing in the air like an old gun dog."

"Then what, Captain?"

"We'll slide the bastard towards the catching bay doors."

"Aye, Captain," Driff replied, tapping in a series of commands.

Dropping the anchors as instructed, Driff forced the front of the ship to point upwards at the water's surface. Sliding backwards, the worm hit the sturdy metal doors with a loud thud. Pinned down by a combination of the ship's forward velocity and the forty-degree angle, it angrily tried to move forward, but it couldn't right its own body to attack.

"Now, Driff. Open the doors and flush the bastard."

Opening wide, the worm and Ritti's corpse both shot out of the rear catching bay doors, carried away into the murky waters, disappearing forever into the depths. In unison, the crew cheered despite the moment being bittersweet - they'd rid themselves of the worm, but they'd lost Ritti, who now wouldn't receive a proper send off.

"Driff, let's get out of here and get paid, shall we?"

Once the Dee-Alma had sailed a few kilometres away from any apparent danger, Ferrago had his wounds tended to by the chief medical officer, Dr

A Small Book

Lukman. Shortly afterwards, he'd been given the greenlight to leave the med bay, so he visited the three worms frozen in stasis, and he smiled to himself.

Without warning, the ship violently shook, launching Cerso across the catching bay. Impacting against the stairwell's guard rail, he lay winded and concussed. Aware they were now under attack from yet another outside threat, Ferrago dashed to help Cerso. Darting down the metal staircase from the upper level, he saw Cerso crumpled on the floor. "Move yourself, Cerso. You can take a nap later. I need you on the deck. Now," Ferrago told his dazed crew member.

Hauling his bulky, muscular frame up off the floor, part coherent, Cerso appeared to be able to carry on, no medical assistance would be necessary, Ferrago hoped. "What was that, Captain? Is the worm back? I thought we'd flushed the bastard?"

Before Ferrago could answer, he spotted a patch of the worm's purple blood on Cerso's shirt. Without warning, Cerso screamed out in agony and collapsed onto his back, in the same way Ritti had, earlier. Brutally burrowing out of Cerso's gut, a baby worm moved hungrily towards Ferrago; both his comfort level and patience began to fray. Determined to stay alive, he dodged the new threat, which in turn took his attention away from the horror show, he'd just witnessed. At that exact moment, his breast plate lit up as Driff reached out to him over the comms. "Captain, we have a BIG problem. There's a fifty-footer approaching now," Driff dutifully informed his captain. "If it latches onto the hull, we won't have enough power to free ourselves."

"Divert power to the thrusters by twenty percent and out run it."

Hitting top speed, the Dee-Alma kept a steady distance from its would-be attacker - the fifty-foot worm with steel plate-like skin and teeth as sharp as the samurai swords he'd seen in the Earth Museum, back on Tellus One.

"Captain, I'm monitoring your situation. Is Cerso's dead?" Driff asked, hoping to hear good news.

"Aye. There was a worm inside him, like with Ritti. One of these things just burrowed its way out of his stomach, and it's growing already," Ferrago advised his trusted first officer and second in command.

"What's the plan, Captain?"

"Simple. We kill it," Ferrago snarled, ready to do whatever necessary to protect his ship and crew. "But Driff, listen to me, this is important - anyone that's had contact with, or has been near one of these bastards, needs to be securely isolated. I fear others might already be incubators for these creatures."

"How so, Captain?"

A Small Book

"They get inside the body, somehow. Maybe it's be their blood making contact with our skin, but I can't be sure. Not yet, anyway."

"What now, Captain?"

"I don't know how many of us could be knocked up, Driff, so I need you to get all the possibly compromised crew members to the med bay and seal them in. We're to adhere to the strictest quarantine conditions."

"Until when, Captain?"

"Until I confirm otherwise," Ferrago confirmed with a nod of his head.

"But, that's most of us, Captain," Driff reasoned. "Operationally, it'll leave us short."

"Meaning what, exactly?"

"It's simple, Captain - we won't be able to function if we're all quarantined."

"Then, we're all on borrowed time, Driff. We either fight now or wait to die. Now, if you'll excuse me for a moment, I've got a little problem here to deal with."

Unsheathing his Dimerian machete from its sheath, strapped to his right thigh, Ferrago brought the razor-sharp blade down hard on the worm. Splitting it's grizzly head in two, he luckily, avoided any splash back of worm blood. Dropping his contaminated machete on the floor, he sprinted back up the stairwell. When he could retrieve and clean his favourite weapon, he would, if he lived to see that long, he told himself.

51

Arriving at the main computer terminal on the deck, he growled at Ari to vacate his seat of control. "Move it, son. I'm taking over."

Loyal to his captain, Ari trusted him implicitly. Willingly vacating his seat, he watched Ferrago flick various switches and tap commands into the control desk keyboard. "Driff, how are we getting on?" Ferrago asked, glancing over his shoulder at Driff.

"It's closed the gap, Captain. We were five hundred meters clear, we're now at two fifty. If we carry on at our current pace, and if that thing doesn't tire, it'll make contact within minutes."

"I've got an idea," Ferrago stated, appearing typically confident to his dutiful crew.

Moving from Ari's station to the vacant seat to his left, he brought up the ship's weapon systems on the main screen. Tapping in a series of complex commands, he diverted the kinetic energy the ship had collected, during the course of its journey, to its outer frame.

Waiting for the energy levels to reach their maximum seemed to take an eternity, when seconds were precious. Moments later, the Dee-Alma was armed and ready to expel the charge in two separate blasts, at the most opportune of moments. Hovering his index finger over the necessary control key, Ferrago began the countdown, from

A Small Book

five to zero; the crew watched on with bated breath.

Seconds later, the worm had finally chased them down. Aggressively attaching itself to the hull, Ferrago recognised the perfect moment to send the first kinetic energy current through the water, hoping to cook the worm from the inside out.

"Twenty years, we've been together, and you haven't let me down", he whispered, communicating privately with his precious vessel, his most treasured worldly possession. "Don't let me down and I'll get you a new power core and paint job on Tellus Six. I promise. How's that sound?"

Pressing down on the control key, the ship emitted the first blast, but the giant worm didn't bite. Instead, it repeatedly struck the hull, causing heavy dents to the outer paneling and minor damage to the tough Becsium framework behind it.

"Captain, the first attack's failed and I'm seeing more worms approach. They're strategically surrounding us. What now, sir?"

"What's the integrity of the hull looking like?"

"We're taking a heavy beating. We won't survive much longer, sir," Driff grimaced.

"Channel all power to the rear thrusters and get us out of here, Driff. We've got what we came for. Mostly. Take off."

The ship began to lift out of the water but couldn't get any real distance without struggling because of the added weight of the worm, which hadn't been factored into Ferrago's plan off escape. With his finger still over the button to drop the other charge, Ferrago waited for the worm to bite down on the ship's outer framework, and it did. Pressing down on the control key again, he released the second and final kinetic charge, taking - literally, his final throw of the dice.

Boom.

Lighting up the worm with a cobalt-blue glow, Ferrago had hit the literal jackpot. Falling like a stone into the murky, violent water below, Ferrago and his crew were all fixed on the main monitor, watching the worm sink beneath the deep, dark depths of the waves. Cheering like the motley crew they were, they'd rightly assumed it'd perished.

From nowhere, the worm rose from the water again with an unsurprising grace, raging and more dangerous than ever. Pushing itself out of the water, it reattached itself and its teeth to the hull. The ship began to fall from the sky.

"Full power to the thrusters, Driff!" Ferrago desperately demanded.

"Aye, Captain," Driff replied, engaging the thrusters. Putting unfair pressure on the Dee-Alma's engine system prompted the warning light to flash on

A Small Book

Driff's screen. Frantically, the remaining engineering crew began to make on the spot repairs as copious amounts of coolant gas escaped from pipes throughout the bay area.

Back on the deck, sparks flew from everywhere, as the worm's grip tightened. As calm as a Volut Batian cow throughout all of the chaos, Ferrago recalled a job on Corbin V, when he'd faced off against a nest of enormous Elaxion Thorn Bugs and won against the odds. Drawing fuel from the ship's fuel line, he recalled how he'd slowly pumped the bugs' network of caves with a highly-flammable chemical. Waiting until the last possible second, he lit his last cigar and dropped it into the nest's entrance, and watched it burn.

"Captain," Driff urgently cried out. "What are your orders?"

Snapping Ferrago out of his memory, he instinctively began to formulate a plan. "Get me a live feed to the bay. Audio, too."

Bringing up the events in the bay, on the main screen, both men saw the damage increase and unfold in real time. The moans and groans of the ship and menacing sound of a metal wire snapping filled them both with dread. As if in slow motion, they watched on as one of the cryo canisters came loose and fell. Fear bounced around Ferrago's mind when the canister hit the corner of a metal storage unit. Ricocheting around the bay, a cyan blue liquid shot out of the pierced cannister and hit Arnine, one of the ship's engineering crew. Covering the engineer from the hip down, his screams of pain filled the bay as his legs turned to ice and fell to pieces. Throughout the screams, Ferrago had an idea. Activating the comms to the bay, he began to put his plan into action. "Gentleman, begin moving the remaining cryo cannisters to the middle of the bay, I'm on my way there, now. We have enough to hold the worms we have on ice in stasis."

"Are we going to do what we did on Kensi Prime, Captain?" Driff asked.

"No. Corbin V."

"Captain, that won't work. Flames required oxygenation. The waves will drown out the flames."

"We won't be burning the waves or the worms."

Driff appeared confused.

"It'll take expert timing. Once it happens, we will have a small window to get out of range of the worms. Trust me, this plan WILL work."

"Why would I ever doubt you, sir? Where do you need me?"

"I need you to helm the ship, and keep us all alive. Route five percent of our fuel to the bay's storage drums."

"Aye, Captain."

A Small Book

Making his way to the lower level via the armoury, Ferrago could hear the continued sound of Arnine's bone-chilling screams of sheer pain and agony. Still, he ordered the crew like a conductor would his orchestra. Instructing they stand the cannisters facing upwards, he had his men use the thick Morkarri storage straps to tie the cannisters together; they worked in total unison. The straps weren't cheap and were just strong enough to serve the desired purpose. Made from the silk of the Morkarri worm, he could always purchase more, he told himself, when he'd next take in a weekend trip on Tellus Four.

In the centre of the bay, where the cannisters sat, Ferrago's hand reached for the pulse cannon, he'd collected on his way to the bay, and clipped it on his belt. "Clear the bay doors and strap yourselves in, this will be one hell of an escape. I'll be the one to take the shot, it's all on me. Driff, when I fire, you hit the thrusters."

"What about your arm, Captain? Can we help strap you in?"

"Driff, your concern is noted but I'll be fine!"

Filled with an adrenaline rush and his one good arm still functioning to a worthy level, Ferrago slid down the ladders into the bay area, just as his men were climbing out. Meanwhile, the worm continued to wrestle the ship into further submission, so he understood he had one last crack shot. Pride alone, he wouldn't allow him to show his men his struggles with the harness, but he managed to secure himself, nonetheless. Injured and exhausted, he stood in front of the bay doors.

Ready to taste victory or experience the bitter taste of ending defeat, he'd hoped to forever avoid, Ferrago activated his comms with his crew on an open line so they could all hear him. Then, tapping a second touch-sensitive control he brought to life his augmented cybernetic eye piece to help guide him with his shot.

At a safe enough distance to carry out his task, he focused his eye piece on the cannisters. Aiming the pulse cannon at the target before him, through the digital crosshairs, he readied himself. "Open the bay doors, Driff."

As the rear bay doors, lined with reinforced Becsium polymer, opened, Ferrago kept his focus fixed firmly on the cryo cannisters, in particular, the one in the middle carrying the ID 1138. Ready, he pulled the pulse cannon's trigger.

Boom.

Echoing deafeningly around the bay, the sound of the cannon made his ears throb. The blast, meanwhile, flew through the chaos, above the water, and impacted with the cannisters, igniting their pressurised load.

Contained by the fireproof bay walls, the explosion

A Small Book

shot out of the open bay doors and lit up the space between the waves and the Dee-Alma. Whilst not advisable, he knew his ship could structurally handle the heat and such a huge ask.

For a fleeting moment, through the flickering flames, he saw the sheer number of worms had grown. Circling in the waves below, Ferrago waited for the lightshow to fade and the heat to subside. Looking down at the worms, he took immense satisfaction from seeing his gamble had paid off - the waves and the worms near the surface began to freeze.

As the artic blast travelled outwards, through the bay doors, it caught the worm attached to the hull. With his hand pressed against the ship's wall, Ferrago sensed the worm's grip had loosened. On her last bit of juice, the Dee-Alma gave all she had left; a thrust of the engines and they were finally free of the worm's hold. Another engine boost later and they were away and soaring into the night sky.

Over the days that followed, the crew patched up the ship and each other, whilst Ferrago took the time to visit the cryo chambers - his reflection showed his arm in a sling. Despite his own pain, his thoughts went to the men who'd lost their lives. 'They know what they're signing up for, but the loss is still a loss,' he told himself.

Heading back to the deck to resume his command,

A D Small

Ferrago could rest easier knowing the payment they'd receive on Tellus Six would pay the crew's wages, he could get a new arm and fix the ship as promised. Most comforting though, the fallen crew's family would each receive a substantial payment, though it'd never be compensation enough for their respective losses.

X Marks the Spot

As the early morning sun beamed through the small window. An amber glow blinded the young twins Nicholas and Noel as they climbed clumsily into the attic. The noise didn't break the Sandman's spell over the rest of the house. They navigated the minefield of loose floorboards, through the items long forgotten by the family. In the thick grey dust, they found footprints, leading them to a stack of boxes stood against the chimney wall. As they struggled to lift one marked last year's Xmas decorations, their father's voice bellowed through the attic floor.

"You won't find them there, boys!"

The Cat

Sauntering out from the shadows, the cat slinked silently passed a wire mesh gate, moving towards the dirty dustbins and stacks of rain-damaged cardboard boxes. Flickering overhead, the streetlight brought to life both the cat's predatory physique and charcoal-coloured fur. Admiring its own reflection in a nearby puddle, the cat tilted its head, curiously.

A scraping sound echoed down the silent street. The cat turned and focused on the darkness. Breaking the surface of the puddle with its front paw, it coiled itself like a spring, ready to attack. Scanning the shadows, it sniffed the air. Stepping back, its eyes widened with fear and its little heart violently thumped.

A burly man in a dirty grey overall limped from the darkness. As he placed a rusty metal cage on the floor, he wiped the sweat from his brow before he covered his greasy black hair with a red weathered baseball cap. He adjusted the long pole with both hands; the steel loop glistened in the moonlight. As the man stepped slowly forward across the patchwork tarmac. The cat saw the metal frame wrapped around his lower leg.

The man placed a cloth mask over his mouth as he opened a small package. He sprinkled the content around the outside of the cage before putting some inside the metal frame. The smell travelled slowly down the street; it became intoxicating. Its nose began to twitch so it stepped back until its hind legs hit the stone wall. The screeching sound of the metal as it scraped across the floor echoed down the street and cut through the hustle and bustle of the town past the wall. The cats' ears pricked up as it heard the calls of its feline family. So it let out the biggest "Meow" it could muster. From beyond the wall a cacophony of cries called back. Again, the cat coiled ready to attack.

Small bags of cat nip hit the floor as the man walked down the street. As the last bag left his hand, he pulled the large pole from his back ready to catch its next victim. The pungent aroma travelled, tricking the cat into thoughts of rolling around in it, but not today. It looked beyond the man into the deep blanket of darkness. The lesser of two evils, fight the man or head into the unknown. A choice to make but the thoughts

A Small Book

of ones lost to the pound, so many taken and never returned. It didn't want to be another.

As the man edged closer the cat took its chance, it feigned right then darted left. This caused the man to lose his balance and began to pirouette like an uncoordinated ballet dancer. The cat ran around the man again causing his good leg to buckle. As he slipped the pole flew up and then came crashing down on his head.

"Arghh!"

Blood trickled down the man's face from the cut on his head, but he had two hands wrapped around his left knee as he writhed on the floor. The cat bolted. It slowed as it trudged through the thick aroma of the catnip towards the boxes; fighting the urge to get lost in the smell. Through the puddle under the broken light, no time to look back must keep going. As the heavens opened the boxes crumbled as the cat climbed. With no time to second guess the cat cleared the mesh gate and landed like a superhero before sauntering into the shadows.

Face the Wall

"Lights out on level 4, Frank."

Darkness devoured the light inch by inch through the west wing. As Corey sat on the edge of his bed, he stared into the mirror and examined his face. He removed the plasters and gauze to reveal some new scars. A bruise on the side of his face resembled an image of a constellation and galaxy beyond the confines of the prison walls. He placed the base of his thumbs on either side of his nose and twisted fast, the pop eased his breathing. The beating he received had been the worst one ever. Memories scarred into his mind began to replay.

Cornered in the shower, fists rained down like fairground mallets. Warm blood poured from his nose and across his swollen lip. He heard his ribs crack with each kick and punch he received. A voice pulled him back to the present.

"You're mine, Boy."

The words echoed around the west wing. Slowly Corey backed himself into the corner of his cell. He wanted to leave this place and he only had two options. One in a body bag or by a miracle. With his bandaged hand he reached for a hole in his mattress and pulled out a piece of a bed spring stuck into a broken toothbrush handle. He pressed it hard against his wrist. Just a little more is all it would take he thought.

"I will get you, boy."

"One more outburst, Myers. You will be thrown in solitary."

He placed the self-made blade back into his mattress. His mind raced as he lay on the bed. How to get himself thrown into solitary? A low thumping sound ran through his thoughts, every beat getting louder. Even as his head throbbed, he soon drifted off to the realm of the sandman.

Bang!

The cell door opened, Corey sat up and looked in the mirror. The skin still sore and tender to the touch,

A Small Book

but the bruise now had a tint of black form around the edge. His head ached, like a thousand cell doors being repeatedly slammed shut. He saw the other inmates as they left their cells. As Corey stepped out onto the walkway and looked down to the next level. With his tattooed tears falling from his eyes, stood Myers, surrounded by his goons. Each one had the gang markings etched on their skin; a crescent moon next to three stars.

They all kept their heads down as they cautiously moved something between them out of the view of the guards. The warden knew things like this happened but unless they were caught in the act, he couldn't do anything. As Corey carefully watched the group, he knew the shiv had his name on it. It finally, landed in Kane's hand, who had a bulky frame covered with tribal markings. On his right arm he had an unfinished sleeve of skulls, each one representing a hit he completed on a fellow inmate. Amongst the skulls sat an armless clock. His eyes moved back to Myers who moved his fingers across his throat and pointed to Corey.

"What's on the menu today, Chef?"
"Same as yesterday, kid."

A D Small

Great, Corey thought, the bacon resembled tough leather.

The only good thing and something which made Friday his favourite day of the week; the scrambled eggs as they were just like how his mother used to make them. It would be the only thing he could eat. He saw Chef move backwards. So he ate a mouthful of the eggs, for a moment he drifted back to being a kid. With every movement, his jaw ached. As he dropped the fork, he grabbed the metal cup and turned to face Kane. His bulky frame blotted out the light with every step he took, but something glistened in his hands. As Kane lunged forward, Corey sidestepped and swung the cup. Crack. The burly frame of Kane wavered then fell like a great Redwood. The inmates gathered like kids in a playground, with every punch thrown the chants got louder and louder.

"Fight...fight... get him... kill him... go on!"

Blood formed around Kane's prone body. The crowd parted as guards in riot gear entered the canteen swinging their batons like gladiators. Some inmates turned and squared ready to fight. Bang! Bang! Another guard appeared from a door with a gun aimed to the ceiling. Everybody dropped to the floor, except for a small group. They blocked the path to Corey and Kane. More guards came into the canteen and collec-

70

tively they all moved towards the small group of inmates. Another lacky, with a face full of tattoos from Myers's gang named Malone received the go ahead from his leader, so he attacked the oncoming guards. He screamed like a warrior going into battle, he dodged a baton from one guard as he wrestled another to the ground. During the commotion Myers turned and saw Corey stood in his red stained prison overalls with a bent metal cup in his hand, soaked in Kane's blood.

Once the guards brought order to the chaos, they wheeled Kane on a stretcher to the infirmary and escorted Corey to the safe place he wanted to be in.

"That's one week for you."

As he walked down the corridor, he could hear the words from Myers fade. Solitary confinement had been placed in the North wing just passed the infirmary. A guard escorted Corey towards cell eight and opened the door with a large key. He heard the lock click and the door pop. Once inside the cell, the guard slammed the door shut. He leant against the wall and slid down to the ground. One week of safety. As the thought ran through his head, Corey let out a big sigh. But he could hear a faint thumping sound coming from the wall. He knew cells seven and nine either side of his were empty.

As he heard the guards' footsteps, Corey dropped his legs to the floor. Then the tray came through the service hatch, this indicated day three of being in solitary. Hot grits with butter, two eggs, two sausages, and two slices of fresh toast. But again the faint thumping sound could be heard, and it worried him as it had got louder since his first night in solitary. He wondered if another inmate wanted to communicate with his gang, using the pipes which wove through this place like a spider's web. He did not know who occupied the other cells, but solitary can affect the sanity of men. The thumping started to change into a familiar sound.

Tick, tock.

But he could not recall seeing a clock on the wall as he entered solitary. The sound echoed around his cell as is eyes scanned to pinpoint its location. He looked near the sink, toilet and under the bed. But he couldn't see anything, so he lay down and rested his head on the pillow. The ticking had not stopped, it had got louder. He couldn't be the only one to hear this. A knock at the door came followed by a stern voice.

"Tray!"

Quickly, Corey placed the tray through the service hatch.

"Can you hear that thumping, a constant banging."

"I can't but this place is as old as time," he chuckled.

Tick, tock.

Again it echoed around the cell. But the guard shut the service hatch and walked away. He had only been in solitary for three days now, he couldn't be losing his mind already. But as he leant against the wall, he heard the ticking clearly. It had to be behind the wall.

He woke to the guard thumping the door of another cell. Another tray of hot grits with butter, two eggs, two sausages, and two slices of fresh toast. With each mouthful he devoured, the ticking got louder and louder. As he swallowed the last fork full, he threw the tray into the corner; it hit the wall. The brick had split, and a chunk sat dislodged from the wall. As he placed the brick on the floor, he reached inside. Slowly he moved his hand around, his finger caught the edge of something there, but it sat just out of reach. Lying flat on the floor, he tried again. Just a little bit more he thought. Then he heard Marcus starting his cell checks. He had been a prison guard for years. After an incident with an inmate, a reshuffle of the guards happened, and he had been moved permanently to the solitary wing.

He barked orders at inmates. But he had been off for the last few days.

Thud!

"You bastard... you broke my fucking fingers."

"If you don't shut your mouth, it won't be the only thing I break."

Another door clicked shut and footsteps echoed the corridor, Marcus moved through the cells like Genghis Khan. One more stretch. Click went the lock. He slotted the brick back and headed for the sink. The cell door opened.

"Face the wall."

Corey turned to check on the wall.

"What you staring at? Turn the fuck around."

"Yes, Sir"

Using a baton Marcus slammed and pinned Corey to the wall, then he scanned the room.

"Don't test me, Boy. You're in my domain now."

He noticed the food tray in the corner.

"What is this?"

"Can you not hear that ticking?"

As Marcus picked up the tray, Corey held his breath. But he hadn't noticed the dislodged brick.

"Three days in and your sanity is slipping," chuckled Marcus.

"I can hear it now."

The tray flew towards the door, Marcus grabbed Corey and thrusted his baton into his gut.

"Remember I am the boss in here."

He left the cell and slammed the door behind him.

The guards called lights out, Corey made his way to the corner of the cell. He removed the brick and again lay flat against the floor. As he slid his arm inside, he managed to gain the reach and pulled the item and his arm free. A tight squeeze through the hole in the wall, but then he replaced the broken brick. He sat on the edge of his bed and held it up to the moonlight coming through the small window in the ceiling. A wooden box with strange markings on each side. No visible clasp or lock. He ran his fingers along each side, systematically covering each section and edge. As he turned it around and around his Anger grew, but with no outlet he placed it on the edge of the bed and walked to the sink. He splashed water on his face and pondered as to what it could be.

The markings had to mean something. As he stood over it, droplets of water fell from his brow onto the box. He watched it as water travelled through the grooves then disappeared. He raised the box to the light and saw a small section which now looked out of place. As he turned the box, he noticed a few more markings on the opposite side.

Nothing happened as he pressed each side individually but when pressed collectively a panel moved, it revealed a small silk pouch. As he undid the string knot, he found inside an old pocket watch. The box then resealed itself. A thought came to him about the box, and he knew he did not need it, so he placed it back in the hole.

He lay there on his bed and stared at the watch. As he looked at the intertwined spiral pattern, it caused him to fall into a hypnotic trance; it had no beginning or end. Light bounced off it creating a glow like the northern lights. He had never seen a sight more beautiful. The ticking had now stopped and slowly he drifted off to sleep with the watch in his hand.

His last day in solitary; but he wanted to stay safe. As he stood there with his hands and legs bound in chains.

"You're fucking history, Boy."

He recognised Kane's voice; he must have got himself thrown into solitary to send me a warning.

A Small Book

His week in solitary had ended. Now the nightmare returns. Guards escorted him back to his cell, he could see Myers and his goons gathered around a table, all of them pulled their finger across their throats before they pointed at him. The guard locked his cell door once he stepped inside.

Wonder wedged in Corey's mind. Where did the watch come from? Who made it? Who put it behind the wall? The questions cycled through his mind as he lay on the bed.

"Lights out on, level four."

He closed his eyes as the sandman called to him.

Silence broken by the noise which had started when he entered solitary.

Tick, tock.

His eyes scanned around his cell for the watch. As the ticking gained more volume Corey found it at the bottom of the bed. He ran his fingers over it, as with the box it had no obvious opening or clasp. As he gazed

77

at the swirling patterns, he fumbled it between his hands. Then it opened. The face of the watch revealed similar markings to the outside. It resembled a watch but one he hadn't seen before; it had four oval shaped holes set at 12, 3,6 and 9. A piece of metal moulded into a figure of eight moved like the hands of a clock. But inside the holes, patterns disappeared and reappeared.

Tick, tock.

There seemed to be a sequence repeating in the patterns. As they changed, he pondered whether it counted up or down. Then one of the ovals turned blank.

The sun beamed through the canteen window and caught the watch as he rolled it around in his hands. When a voice snapped him from his trance, Corey concealed the watch in his pocket.

"What you got there, Boy?"

"Nothing for you, Myers."

He tucked the watch back in his pocket as Myers and his gang moved around the table. Two of his goons stood either side of Corey.

"Give me that."

"No!"

A Small Book

"Seems like you found your balls in solitary?"

"Like you give a shit!"

"Just give it to me and we can call it square."

"Do I look like a fucking idiot?"

"You will be a fucking dead one!"

As Corey stood up a hand pushed him back down. He looked up at the goon named Dale.

"Do you remember what happened to Kane?"

As Corey stood, he shifted his weight and at the same time he grabbed the arm of Dale. With a swift motion Corey twisted the arm and then slammed Dale into the table. Another goon stepped forward, but Myers shook his head and lowered his hand. As the guards approached; Myers laughed and placed his hand on Corey's back.

"What's going on here?"

"Nothing, Boss. We are just having a laugh at his expense."

Pointing towards his fallen goon slumped on the table.

"I will be watching the both of you."

Once the guard had moved away, Corey pulled away from Myers. As he walked back to the cell, he glanced at the watch. Another oval had turned blank, it must be a countdown, he thought. As he approached his cell Corey spotted someone leaving it. There would be no point informing the guards or warden, he knew each guard took a bribe of some kind. Inmates' deaths chalked up as freak accidents. He sat on the bed and looked in his mirror; a message read 'dead by daybreak.'

Tick, Tock.

With a mind full of turmoil, Corey sat entranced by the watch as a third oval turned blank. It had to be counting down he thought. But anticipation ripped through his mind as he paced his cell. The ticking got louder. Then he heard footsteps and voices. So he stood still near the back wall.

"8 minutes till Frank gets back."

He walked to the sink; Corey needed to give himself room to have a chance of surviving the night. Then he heard Myers.

"If you hand it over I might, just might let you live."

The last oval turned blank as Corey glanced at the watch.

"If you want it, come and get it."

As he rolled his sleeves up, Myers pushed Kane out of the cell.

"I was hoping you would say that!"

Death stood at the door, thought Corey. His eyes

A Small Book

dropped to watch Myers hands as he expected a shank. But a look of disbelief filled his face as Myers threw a right hook to the side of his head. Now the rules have been set, so he dropped his shoulder and punched Myer's in the gut. He watched as Myer's reeled and staggered, but then he froze in mid-fall. As Corey looked around, he saw everyone motionless, as if captured in a photograph.

A big white flash lit up the west wing, the noise sounded like a symphony of cogs moving in sync. Thinking he had lost his mind, he stepped out of his cell, and everything sat motionless, he followed the light around the corner.

"Hi, Corey."

Bewildered to find an old man in front of him. Who wore a white suit with a neatly trimmed white, grey beard standing against the guardrail. On his jacket's lapel, sat a pin in the shape of a figure of eight. The old man looked over the thin wire rims of his glasses at Corey.

"Who are ... How do you know?"

"Mr Corone is my name. Let's just say I know all I need to know about you."

"Impossible, I have never met you."

"That is true you have not, but I have been watching you for some time now."

"This is crazy, I must be dreaming."

A D Small

"You're quite sane, and as you can see."

The old man leaned into Corey and nipped him.

"Hey, hey."

"So you felt it then?" chuckled Mr Corone.

"What do you want with me? How did you get in here?"

A white glow surrounded Mr Corone, so bright it lit up the surrounding cells. As he took a look inside, he saw inmates frozen like statues.

"I am here to offer you a way out. Only the walls of time can hold me."

"Impossible; If I survive tonight, I am here for a while."

"I can free you from this place, away from Myers and the beatings. I am offering you the chance of your lifetime."

As Corey, looked back into the cell he occupied. He could not believe what he saw at the back of the cell, a version of himself frozen.

"What the hell is going on? Who are you actually?"

"I am to time, what mother is to nature."

"Father...."

"Yes, Corey. I have frozen the world. Part of what I can do."

"Why have you come to me with this offer?"

"I have seen you throughout your life being a

82

A Small Book

watcher of people. I know you have lost your way. But with this opportunity, it will help you redeem yourself."

"How long have you been doing this job?"

"Honestly... too long. I am exhausted but my time is almost over."

"Do you expect me to believe this?"

"I know deep down inside you yearn for freedom. I can take this life away and give you a second chance. But you have got to want the job I cannot force it upon you.

"Is that your choice?"

"No it is one of the laws of time, there are many more which you will need to learn."

"I haven't decided yet, I feel like I am losing my mind."

"You leave me no choice but to show you?"

Out of his pocket, Mr Corone pulled out a pocket watch. He then turned and unclasped the watch. A flash of white light appeared, which blinded Corey. As he opened his eyes, they were stood in the showers of the prison. He could see himself standing under the water. Next, Myers and his goons walked in. With no way to escape, Corey watched Kane strike first. But when he noticed the scar on Kane's face, he realised this is yet to come. Blood whirled down the drain as Corey lay there defenceless.

83

"Please no more, I don't want to see this!"

There is another white flash, and they are back on the walkway, time is still frozen.

"You can either stay in this hell or take over the job."

"What's the catch? There has to be one!"

"You become me, is the only catch."

"I can't stay here, what do you need me to do?"

"Do you have the watch?"

He stepped back into his cell and took it from himself. He placed it into Mr Corone's outstretched open hand.

"There will come a time when you need to find a replacement. Choose wisely."

A light emanated from the centre of the watch face and gradually engulfed the darkness as each second passed. As the light dispersed, Corey opened his eyes. Mr Corone had vanished. But as he looked around the prison wing, the world began to slowly move. He panicked as guards ran towards him, but they ran through him, as if he had become a ghost.

He saw the doorway into his cell. The six guards piled in. As he looked through the bars, he saw Myers motionless on the floor. One guard tackled Corey and slammed him into the wall. Then as another joined in, they handcuffed Corey and dragged him out of the cell. Shocked at what had unfolded in front of him.

A Small Book

"What?"

His shackled self, stared directly at him and winked. Something strange came over Corey, as he looked down, he now wore the same suit Mr Corone wore. He turned and pulled a watch from his jacket pocket, as it opened a big flash of white light began to grow. It turned into a circle and as it got bigger, Corey could see giant cogs and springs, it looked like the inside of a watch. As if, looking into the mechanics of time itself. Through the cogs he saw a large window, which held a star system, sprinkled with shining stars. The thunderous ticking, called out to him, the sound that had been following him stopped as he walked through the light. Then the light disappeared.

Midnight Train

Everything rattled as the midnight train passed my home. From my armchair I peered out of the window. I straightened my glasses as I looked up and down the tree line, dust clouds ran up both sides of the tracks. I looked up at the clock, the hands showed 11:00pm.

The Twitching Curtain

As he clambered up the flights of stairs, Roderick kept one hand firmly on the satchel draped over his shoulder. Numbness slowly travelled up to his knees with every step. But he couldn't stop. As he reached the tenth floor he headed through the door and down the dimly lit hallway. Broken lights flickered in time with the thunderstorm which raged above the busy city. Out of his jacket pocket, he removed some paper. He unfolded it to reveal the scribbled address, twenty-two, Saint Dutton Tower. Frantically, he checked the doors as he ran down the hallway. Panic set when he heard footsteps from the stairwell. He pulled the handle down of number twenty-two, but the door wouldn't budge. With his shoulder he leaned against the wooden door, it opened fractionally. He took a deep breath, sucked in his stomach, and attempted to

A D Small

squeeze through the gap. After half a dozen failed attempts and with the footsteps in the stairwell getting louder. He stopped and scanned the hallway. As the storm lit up the sky, he caught his reflection in the window, fear and concern etched across his face. He left the door open, unsure if it would help delay the person who pursued him. As the rain battered the window he tried the latch, it opened, and he let out a silent sigh.

He cautiously climbed out on to the long ledge and slowly shuffled along to the next window. His long jacket became drenched and heavy as he gazed through the thick glass. He saw a grand apartment, filled with clothes rails and boxes, but no sign of life. Why this address, and why the book, Roderick pondered. But he wanted to be a part of the Red Circle, so he had to complete this task. His initiation to be a part of a group he wished he belonged to. He tried to prize the window open, but it would not budge. Cautiously he shuffled to the next window, each step his rain-soaked jacket weighed heavy on his shoulders. The next window opened, and he carefully climbed inside. In a small mirror he caught his reflection. His flowing locks of brown hair clung to his slender face. He removed his jacket and placed it on the floor next to the window. As he held the satchel, he opened the clasp to check the contents; he ran his

A Small Book

finger over the book, it lay there completely bone dry but most of all safe. The enormous room had clusters of boxes stacked between several rows of clothes rails. Along the far wall stood four giant mirrors were screwed into the wall, each one reached from the floor to the ceiling.

As Roderick moved between the rails, he saw each outfit had been protected by plastic covers. One label caught his intrigue, Mr Julius Huddlesworth. He had heard things about him from Mr Garrett. Other names he saw were Miss Paris Bromley, Mr Corben Jones but Roderick hoped to meet Mr Huddlesworth one day. Then the stammering voice of his pursuer echoed down the hall. He had heard of the Mage Runners and their ruthlessness, but he did not want to get close to one to find out.

"You can't hide forever, boy." stammered his pursuer.

Then he heard something being scraped along the wall in the hall. He remembered the conversations with Mr Garrett about the Mage Runners, they had metal gauntlets which they used to harness their Dark Magic. As Roderick removed the satchel from around his neck, he placed it behind one of the mirrors. It balanced perfectly across the two large screws which held the mirror in place. A thud travelled through the door and the voice stuttered.

91

"I will find you, boy. Then you're going to wish I hadn't."

The door opened, Roderick contemplated heading for the window, could he make it in time he thought. His heart pounded, as he waited, crouched behind half a dozen boxes. He saw a hand reach into the room, and it tried to find whatever blocked the door. But someone had cast a spell to create a magical doorstop. Then a dark amethyst glow emanated around the door; before it vibrated violently. The same-coloured light filled the room as splinters of wood scattered like a buckshot. But as footsteps followed, Roderick dropped his hands, he saw the silhouette of a tall man. After the bright light dissipated, it revealed his dark grey suit and black hair slicked back, wearing horn rimmed glasses. A metal gauntlet attached to his right arm; all six rings glowed as they rotated around. He watched the Mage Runner point his hand forward. A hum grew louder and louder, then something invisible tightened around Roderick. As much as he fought, he could not stay hidden, whatever held him controlled him like a puppet. A weightlessness fell over him as he began to levitate. The Mage Runner approached, paused for a moment, and tilted his head before he pulled his hand back and Roderick floated towards him.

"Where is it, Boy!", he sputtered

With his lips locked tight Roderick tried to clog his

A Small Book

mind with random thoughts, just like Mr Garrett had taught him. He had to cover up the day's events. As he looked at the mage, he saw the twitch in his left eye, this along with the stammer made him look laughable to the ordinary person, but not Roderick.

"You will tell me!", he said with a stammer.

The Mage removed a black gem from his jacket. It sat encased in a metal frame; it glistened as the lightning storm filled the night sky. The thunder rattled the windows of the building. A sharp pain filled Roderick's chest as the Mage placed the gem on his flesh. His focus slipped away, as the pain ramped up to an unbearable level, but the Mage just laughed and stumbled over his words.

"You can't hold out; your body and spirit will break."

A montage of the meeting with Mr Garrett and the taking of the book flashed across Roderick's mind, intermittently at first then more as the pain worsened. The object could not fall back into the hands of Solomon Parker, the darkest and cruellest of all mages. He closed his eyes, dug deep for more strength, and pushed the memories back. Footsteps filled the room. As he opened his eyes, he saw a well-built bearded man, in a long, worn winter coat, dart past him. The Mage Runner recoiled as a blue spark of energy bounced at the spot he once occupied, he then

93

muttered something under his breath and threw his hand forward.

A rally of purple amethyst and blue azure blasts bounced across the room. Each one landed closer than the last. The bearded man fired another shot of what looked like lightning, but Roderick noticed the blasts emanated from a small glass ball, which he held tightly in his soup bowl sized hand. As the bearded man turned around, he stood in awe as he gazed into the man's empty eye socket. Mr Garrett said anything could be used as a magical conduit. The bond around Roderick weakened, his eyes scanned the floor, to judge his fall before he hit the ground.

A hand reached down and pulled him to his feet, even as the battle continued in front of them. As Roderick steadied himself, he saw Mr Garratt in a smart light grey suit, with a grey goatee, all neatly trimmed, his hair parted down the middle. He resembled a Wall Street trader.

"Well done, Kid. I knew you had potential."

"Thanks. Who is that guy?" asked Roderick.

"Well, sport. Mr Parker as called upon one of his top Runners, to catch you. Peter Friday, is his name."

They both turned and watched the two remaining mirrors. The surface of them both rippled like a pebble breaking the surface of a pond. Two figures then appeared slowly and walked towards them; Mr Garrett

A Small Book

turned to them both and gave a slight nod. But Roderick stayed quiet.

The woman with red hair held up by a large clip, opened her jacket and revealed her purple dress which clung to her slender figure. She reached inside and pulled out a pair of knitting needles then looked at the other man who had entered the room with her, he gave her a nod. The tall man who had a head of grey hair, looked towards the ongoing battle as bolts of energy hit the walls around them. He then turned to Mr Garrett and said, "Did he acquire the object, Eugene?"

Mr Garrett turned and looked at Roderick.

"Did you get it?"

"I did, who is he?"

"Kid he is the one the only, Julius Huddlesworth."

He didn't need to be told, Roderick ran to the mirror, reached around for the satchel, and handed it to Mr Huddlesworth. Even in the chaos, excitement filled his body.

"Thanks for this my boy, you have got a valuable skill set."

"What did I steal?"

"You didn't steal anything; it is the complete opposite you have retrieved something of mine. Something which hasn't been in my possession for over 20 years, so I thank you."

95

A D Small

"I know you wanted me to get it back but why didn't you just storm the building?"

Before Roderick got his answer, the large, bearded man took a bolt of energy to the chest, which sent him through the air, into a bunch of boxes. As Mr Friday adjusted his horn-rimmed glasses, he aimed his gauntlet towards everyone. With his white wolf headed cane held in the air, Mr Huddlesworth stood between Roderick and Mr Friday. The head of the cane began to glow a bright orange.

"Now Paris!" said Mr Huddlesworth to the red-haired woman.

With eyes transfixed, Roderick gazed as Paris separated her two knitting needles, with one in each hand she hurled multiple blasts of energy. He tried to deflect her blasts, but Mr Friday struggled and staggered backward. As this battled ensued, Mr Huddlesworth turned around.

"Open the portal now, Eugene!"

From his pocket Mr Garrett removed his mobile phone and hit a button. Before he looked up one of the large mirrors started to ripple like a pond.

"Ready, Julius!" said Mr Garrett.

"Come on Corben on your feet." said Mr Huddlesworth to the bearded man who lay on the floor.

Wide eyed with awe at how Mr Huddlesworth

96

A Small Book

organised his coven. He hoped to be a part of it one day. They all gathered in front of the mirror; but as Roderick stared at the ripples he jumped back. As he surveyed it again, he saw a round bearded face. A hand touched his shoulder as he turned and looked at Mr Garrett.

"What's wrong Roderick?"

"I saw something in the..."

"That would be Mr Hogan, you will meet him soon. Be ready to jump into the mirror when I tell you to, ok."

He acknowledged the instruction as he looked across the room. With his gauntlet glowing, Mr Friday ran towards them, blasts of energy left his hand. One hit the wall above Roderick's head and caused debris to hit the floor next to him. He saw Corben defend the group using his own bolts of energy. As another barrage of blasts came from Mr Friday, one hit Corben square in the chest and sent him through the air. They all watched as Corben's bulky frame disappeared through the ripple in the mirror. Then a roar came from Mr Friday as he fired more amethyst bolts. But even through the magical light show, Roderick could see the fiery intent in his eyes.

As Roderick ducked one of the bolts, he collapsed into a stack of boxes. He knew Mr Friday would not stop. As he stood, he saw through the ripples in the mirror, Mr Hogan helped Corben to his feet. Then they both had an intense argument, but it could not be heard. Again more blasts flew overhead. Then he heard the voice of Mr Garrett.

"Get over here!"

He moved with purpose towards the mirror, but he didn't notice the open box and fell. As he hit the floor, he watched Mr Garrett disappear through the mirror. Energy blasts flew from Paris's knitting needles.

"On your feet, darling!"

As Roderick looked up, he saw the held-out hand of Mr Huddlesworth. They both darted for the mirror. He turned when he heard Mr Huddlesworth again, he shouted words from an ancient language and held his cane in the air with two hands. A glow slowly emanated around them and the mirror like a forcefield. From the gauntlet, Mr Friday removed two small balls and tossed them towards Mr Huddlesworth. They glowed the same colour as his gauntlet; sparks began to interact with the forcefield.

In amazement Roderick watched Mr Huddlesworth fall to one knee. He fought to stand, even as Mr Friday leapt over the rails of clothes. With her knitting needles in hand, Paris moved in front of them both and uttered words in an old language. As the shield collapsed the purple glowing balls flew across the room towards the Mage Runner. They both

A Small Book

watched as the two balls hit the opposite wall and exploded, sending debris in all directions. As the words left her mouth, she aimed both of her needles in Mr Friday's direction as he jumped through the air. A ball of orange light hit Mr Friday. As the brightness intensified Roderick brought both his arms over his face. His blurred vision faded. He then saw a piece of fabric fall onto the clothes rail. As he looked closely the folds in the fabric resembled a curtain. He took a step forward when he noticed what looked like an eye in the pattern flicker.

"Well done, Paris. Now let us get out of here. We got what we came for."

As his jaw dropped, Roderick spun around and looked at Paris who placed her knitting needles inside her jacket.

"You turned him into a curtain!"

"Yes, I did darling, he will be ok, it's not permanent."

As he stepped into the mirror, Roderick looked over his shoulder as the portal closed behind him.

Blackout

For four rounds, I had taken a pummelling off Brad "The Nightmare" Taylor. I can hear the crowds' cheers, but my vision is waning. A barrage of hooks and jabs in the previous rounds had left me with brain fog. Blood trickled from my nose and over my swollen lip as I sat in the corner. Every breath pierced my lungs like the Hans Moretti sword box trick.

Back in the day, this could have been a world title fight, in front of a bustling Wembley crowd, but allegations of substance use crippled Brads career. Now he pounded through all comers in the underground circuit.

As the crazed crowd chanted for more carnage and violence, the referee called us both to the middle of the ring. He checked my gloves and held up his hand.

"How many fingers am I holding up?"

"Three."

"Okay, kid."

Ding, ding. The final round started to emulate the one before. A combination of jabs to the jaw, turned my legs to jelly. I staggered backwards but then Brad caught me in the ribs. As I collapsed, I braced myself on the ropes, a break for sure but nothing to worry about. Every move and breath intensified the pain. The crowd cheered as I managed to block his jab. Could the underdog cause an upset? I threw a wild left hook and missed Brad. Then, everything around me turned black.

The changing room lights flickered as I opened my eyes. As I inhaled, the musky odour of Mr Rogan filled my nostrils. I lifted my head and saw him stood near the door, chatting on his mobile phone. From his side of the conversation he discussed the winnings from the fight and another event in the next few weeks. Three quarters of the underground circuit sat under the watchful eye of Mr Rogan. He had grown his family business into a powerhouse. His successful rise came at a cost with the long scar from his forehead to his jawline. I don't have any visible battle scars to tell

A Small Book

anyone about. Once he finished his call, he turned to face me.

"How's the jaw, kid?"

I grimaced and raised my hand to my face. He signalled for me to stop.

"Going to set up another fight for you once you're healed up, you'll earn lots of cash with me," he promised, dropping a rolled-up wad of notes into my hand, before heading for the door.

As his musky odour left the room, I sat up and took a deep breath, each one caused immense pain. I worked out the pain to cash ratio before every fight and found the pain dispersed quicker when I counted the queen's head. As the door swung shut, Dale entered carrying a bulging army green duffle bag. His deep-set eyes and gaunt face looked at me as he placed the bag on the table. But he couldn't hide the shiver, every couple of seconds he rubbed his arm near his elbow.

"Shit, he fucked you up bad."

I cracked my jaw and tossed him the wad of cash. "You should see the other guy."

His gaunt lifeless face morphed into one of a child on Christmas day, as he caught the money. He sprinted out the door towards his next fix. I turned back towards the mirror and looked at the damage from the fight. With my right hand on my ribs, I took a

A D Small

deep breath and pressed hard. Crack. A sound I have grown accustomed to. I took a deep breath again.

"Good as new."

I dunked my head into the sink and counted to ten, the icy water tightened my skin as it slowly turned a crimson red.

As I threw the blooded towel in my bag, I watched my skin weave back together above my right eye. A first aid box hung from a loose nail above the sink. I rummaged through it and found a gauze patch. The loss needed to be convincing. So I smeared some of my blood on it and placed it above my right eye. Inside my duffle bag sat bundles of fifties wrapped in elastic bands. Knowing the fights outcome is the way you beat the house. The money eased the immediate pain.

The smell of stale piss and rat shit caused me to change my mind on a shower. This fight had earned me a stay in a reasonable hotel with a clean bathroom. Carefully I slipped my hoodie on and made sure not to catch the gauze. As I fastened the buttons on my combats, I heard Mr Rogan and another man in conversation. From the way he spoke- in short, sharp sentences, enunciated correctly – the other man had clear military connections. Cautiously, I held my position. As I peered out through the crack in the door. He introduced himself to Mr Rogan, as General Hewlett.

A Small Book

A name I had never heard before. With both bags over my shoulder, I grabbed my jacket.

As I stood cautiously at the door, the well-spoken General enunciated every word.

"Mr Rogan, I am looking for this man," Hewlett told him, handing over a photograph. "He may go by the name of Carl Nash."

Shocked and stunned as I haven't used or heard the name, Nash, since I travelled around Scotland in the 1950's.

"Well General, can't say that I recognise that face. I see a lot of bruised and battered faces, in my line of business. It isn't suited for pretty boys like that."

I watched as General Hewlett removed his hat with ease and precision, he then stepped around Mr Rogan and headed in my direction.

"My intel is reliable, Mr Rogan, if you continue to impede my assignment, I will be forced to act accordingly."

My gaze crossed to Mr Rogan, and I see him run his finger down the scar on his face. The two of them stood in and old west style stand-off. Each of them trying to decipher the body language of the other.

"I am sorry General, but you need to speak to whoever gave you your intel. Like I said, you won't see pretty boys in this place.

With the military here asking questions about me, I headed out the back door of the building.

Once outside, the rain came down hard and heavy. As I stepped into the hustle and bustle of the streets, I pulled my hood up. The itchiness had stopped, I knew my wound had healed but I had to keep up the act and wince occasionally. All part of the façade I thought. As I approached the crossing an odd-looking man headed my way. Around his neck hung a wooden board with the words 'they are watching you' scrawled in black marker. Before the traffic light had changed the man turned to me.

"They are everywhere!"

He continued ranting to himself as people began to stare. As I turned, I saw his dilated pupils through his thick dirty mahogany hair. Out of nowhere I heard a screech, as I turned to witness a door open on a dark grey transit van. Multiple hands bundled me inside and smothered my face with a rag. The smell burnt my throat, but the more I struggled the weaker I became. As the door slammed shut, I slipped into unconsciousness.

My eyes opened to see a single light gently swinging above my head. As I moved, I realised my wrists and

A Small Book

ankles had been bound to a podiatry chair. More lights activated as the door opened. Once my eyes adjusted, I saw a slender but athletic man push a trolley into the room. The wrinkles on his face and the receding hairline suggested he had to be in his late forties. The years have given me the experience to know a person's age without being told.

"I will be right outside, Doctor Cole."

The silent doctor acknowledged the guard and then sat down and stared at me. I glanced at the trolley covered in a white sheet, which I knew they intended to use on me. But I would play along and have some fun. I asked the usual questions, where am I, you have the wrong person; I am Adam Strauss. The Doctor had a cold gaze. Without hesitation he started to name some of my aliases.

"Carl Nash, Logan James, Marc Calloway, William Pratt. But your real name is Marcus Evans, you were born 1885, in London England. You were declared missing in action in World War One."

He listed the countries I had been spotted in over the last 15 years. In my old age I had become careless. The doctor knew what I could do, and he had the evidence to prove it. My thoughts turned to how to get out and what did they know. The doctor leaned over towards the trolley and uncovered lots of scalpels, needles, and a steel box. He took out a small vile filled

107

with a bright navy coloured liquid and attached it to a needle gun. With one hand he forced my head into the head rest and with his free hand injected the vile into my neck.

"I've been hung, buried, burned, and drowned but this is a new one."

Within moments blood started dripping from my nose, eyes, and mouth. My veins began to burn. Seconds later, just darkness.

As I came around, the screeching sound and a pulsing carmine red light came from the corridor. Something had interrupted the plans of Dr. Cole. But what he wanted and where he had gone, didn't need to be a concern now. I had to get myself free. But two frantic voices and heavy footsteps started to break through the alarm.

"This is a shit show. What the hell do they want?" barked Eddie.

"Not a fucking clue, Dr. Cole wants patient 1908 taken out the back door, asap. So, let's move it." affirmed Marc.

As the door moved, I slumped back in the chair. Over the years the ability to lie motionless and limp had become second nature to me. With my arms

A Small Book

draped over their shoulders they carried me out through the door. A loud explosion echoed through the corridors. Then the alarm and the crimson red lights stopped.

"Come on, Marc, eyes forward!"

"How far now? Cause this guy is getting heavy," exclaimed Marc.

"Down this corridor and to the right." grunted Eddie.

Even with my eyes shut, the cold draft from the exit door swirled down the corridor. Marc took all my weight as Eddie moved forward; I heard him flick the safety off on his gun. As he eased the door open an orange, fluorescent light engulfed the corridor. I kept my eyes closed as they dragged me through the light, but the earthy musky smell filled my nostrils. As my senses were overwhelmed, I didn't hear shots fired, but Eddie hit the floor first then I followed. As I hit the floor, I opened my eyes to see an explosion blow a hole in the roof of the building. The sound and sight of the fire lit the sky. The light show allowed me to roll over and check for an exit. There were no signs of move-ment as I scanned the adjacent treeline. Another explosion set more of the building on fire. I heard screams coming from inside. As I approached a window, I saw a ball of fire flying towards it. As the glass shattered a guard in flames landed on the floor

109

and writhed in pain. Being burned alive sucks in every way. But as I looked at the man in flames, a helplessness washed over me. As his screams filled the night air, something tore through my flesh. I collapsed to the floor, as his screams stopped suddenly. Blood trickled from the hole in his head. A mercy killing or a shooter who didn't want to be haunted by the screams. I picked myself up and ran alongside the building, dozens of blinding lights caused me to stop as I turned the corner. But more than anything the words I heard are what caused me to stop in my tracks.

"Did you really think you could hide from us? Marcus. Your little foray into the boxing circle caught our attention. Thought you would have hidden better than that. Time you went to sleep."

From the shadows stepped Mason Evans, my twin brother. I had not seen him for over thirty years, and I wished I were not seeing him stood before me. But this meeting meant the company had taken him out of stasis. Our mother could never tell us apart, but I know she would be ashamed of him for his actions. I have not been a saint or led a perfect life, but Mason had turned sadistic in his old age, which caused our paths to split. As the lights dimmed, my cold stare mirrored his, our hazel-coloured eyes reflected the hate. His deep brown hair had been military cut which revealed his oval-

A Small Book

shaped face. The gunshot wound in my side had healed so I stood up straight and took a deep breath.

"So, they took you out of your box, dear brother!"

Before the words had left my mouth, Mason tossed something towards me. When I opened my hand, I could see a purple cross medal. Instantly I knew what would happen next.

"Don't you dare, you bastard, don't you fucking dare say it."

"Train carriage, Twin, hometown, effect, eight, fire, sunrise, nineteen, old, worn."

As he spoke the last of the trigger words; I fell into darkness. The nightmare began.

Revelation

Water ran underneath the door, as he pushed it open. He stepped onto the bath mat, but it didn't squelch. The mirror showed him what it had witnessed on this violent night. He looked inside the bathtub; his own lifeless face stared back from the bottom of the bloody water.

The First Book to Fall

Darting down a dimly lit corridor with the book in hand, the dense air sat heavily on Alex's lungs. Charging at the door ahead, he slammed through it with ease, the lock bounced out into the street. Stepping out into the pouring rain, he momentarily glanced back. Had he escaped his pursuer or was it waiting for him in the darkness?

Glancing down at the rare, first edition book with the leather cover, he'd sworn to protect only hours before, Alex's only goals were to protect the book's spirit and to get it to the library. Sprinting towards the junction, a loud, otherworldly scream distracted him. From behind the broken door, the scream grew louder. Pivoting towards the sound, he didn't see the oncoming car. Colliding heavily with the vehicle, Alex landed hard on the wet pavement. Writhing in pain, clutching his knee with one hand, he held the book even tighter with the other. Out of the downpour, he saw the almost human-like creature emerge from the doorway; it dressed like a human and had similar physical traits but still carried many differences.

Wincing as he stood, Alex, ignored the livid driver's anger, refusing to look back. Seconds later, he heard two sets of footsteps closing in on him. Hobbling as fast as his injured body could carry him, every step hurt more than the one before. Limping passed a row of dilapidated shops and restaurants, and their over-flowing refuse bins, the screech rang out again but now, Alex could now only hear his own footsteps.

Turning blindly down an alleyway, Alex prayed the shortcut would bring him to the library, he could almost taste his protected haven. Like a meerkat, with his head firmly on a swivel, he hobbled further down the alleyway, the unsettling sound of his own heartbeat rang around his head. Stopping for a moment to catch his breath, he saw the creature, up close and personal. Fearful, he staggered backwards and tripped over a stray bin bag.

Laid flat out on his back, his injured leg took the brunt of the fall. Composing himself, he hobbled down the alleyway.

Spotting a nearby open door, Alex made his move. Suddenly, as if from nowhere, the creature came into

A Small Book

view. Under the streetlight, its porcelain, ghost-like skin gave it a horrifying appearance; its charcoal-coloured veins, moreso. Fear pinned him to the floor. Stepping forward, the creature didn't try to communicate with him in his prone state, it just breathed slowly and ravenously.

Standing over Alex, the creature ripped the book from his grasp. Opening its mouth widely, it revealed row after row of razor-sharp teeth. Gazing at the book in awe, the creature bit into the leather-bound book, its eyes turning a bright amethyst as it feasted on the book's content, feeding on its soul. Dropping the book to the ground, the pages fell open at the mid-way point. Alex could see all the words had now disappeared. The creature screeched again and lunged at Alex.

The Audition

A black shiny stretched limousine pulled onto the runway of Barrington Airport; its driver slowly navigated the icy tarmac being mindful of the remains from the storm from the night before. As it parked up beside a hangar, the driver climbed out, straightened his jacket, and put on his black chauffeur cap. With haste he moved to the passenger door and opened it, out stepped Louie Howell. He looked the same off screen as he did on screen with his waist-high black pants, white shirt and blonde hair slicked back. Fans of the show, 'Who Got Talent' had labelled him the nasty one, the judge who left all the contestants emotionally scarred since the show's inception with his brutal comments. But the day's auditions had left him drained and more short-tempered than usual.

The acts were flat and lacklustre in Manchester,

with no spark at all. Nothing to rival the winner of last year's competition, the dance sensation, Carolyn Doherty. His next stop, London, for the following weeks show, and he hoped it would produce him another winner of the competition. The storm matched the downward spiral of his mood, he just wanted to go home and get some sleep. Tomorrow, he had a big meeting with two important people regarding plans for a new show. With his private jet ready for the flight, it would not take long to travel back to London. The driver followed Louie and kept him dry from the downpour as they walked towards the jet.

"Have a safe flight, sir."

"Thank you, Argyle. I will be in touch regarding my next Manchester visit. Have a safe journey back. "

"Thank you, sir."

He moved up the steps as Argyle passed the umbrella to the air hostess and ran back to the limousine.

"Good evening, Mr. Howell, I am Denise. The captain has informed me, once you're comfortable and ready, we will take off."

"Thank you. Please, could I have a Gin and Tonic with Ice?"

"No problem, anything else, sir?"

"No that will be all, thank you."

A Small Book

As he stepped through the door, he turned into the seating area. Two single chairs faced each other with a table between them on his left and the same to his right. Beyond those, on either side of the plane were two recliner chairs. He grabbed the first chair on his left, as he sat down, he caught a glimpse of himself in the full-length mirror built into the wall. The reflection showed the tiredness in his eyes. This season of the show had taken its toll on him, but he just could not stop working.

He saw the red light above the toilet door at the back of the cabin and thought it maybe the captain. The soft material of the chair made him loosen up and he unbuttoned his shirt a little. The stress of the day began to drift away. He opened his eyes when he heard the ice as it rattled around the glass. Gracefully Denise moved down the aisle in her black heels, medium length skirt, and a purple blouse. Her walnut-coloured hair held up in a bun with a clip, except for a loose strand which fell down the side of her face.

"Here you go, sir."

"Thank you. Please, tell the Captain, I am ready for take-off. "

"I will sir."

As he slumped in the chair, Louie took a long sip, just what he needed he thought. He took another sip

121

A D Small

as the engines purred. A light above him turned green and the intercom clicked into life.

"This is your captain speaking. Please, can everyone make their way to their seats and strap themselves in ready for take-off."

The hostess moved passed him towards the back of the plane.

"Excuse me this plane was only intended for me. May I ask who else is on this flight?"

"It's only the three of us on this flight. But I will go and see who's in there."

He observed Denise knock on the door, she awkwardly looked back towards him and smiled. His face showed the level of his frustration, by her smile as it slowly faded, she knocked again and spoke.

"You need to come out right now?"

Her shoulders dropped as no answer came and she again turned with an apologetic smile. This delay did not help his mood. He placed his drink on the table with a sigh. As he moved towards the toilet door, he caught a glimpse of the weather through one of the windows, the storm had picked up pace in the brief time he had been on the jet. Impatiently, Louie waved Denise aside and reached for the handle of the door. He pulled it down, nothing happened.

. . .

122

A Small Book

"Come out of there now!! I don't need any further delays."

As Louie rapped the door; Denise hurried to the captain's cabin. Again no response came. Rage began to boil inside of him, and he slammed his fist against the wall. As the toilet door opened, Louie heard ice being rattled in a glass, he expected it to be Denise, but he turned to see a hooded man sat crossed legged on the floor shuffling a deck of cards with one hand. Shocked and unnerved by what Louie could see in front of him, he didn't expect to be strangely intrigued by the situation.

The man placed the glass and the cards on the table. With a wave of his hands the cards disappeared. As the man stood, he removed his hood. Instinctively, Louie checked the man's attire. A very odd combination but his hair style stood out, short, spiked, penny-coloured hair with red streaks in his fringe. He removed his long black weather worn street coat with patches stitched into the fabric; and tossed it onto one of the reclining chairs. Underneath his coat the young man wore a torn Black Sabbath vest over a black t-shirt, his arms covered in tattoos. Around his neck, hung a handful of chains and string with metal and wooden symbols attached to them. Bemused by the brashness, Louie watched as the man made himself at home. He moved cautiously back to his chair, and wondered if

123

Denise would walk in at any moment and eject the young man from the plane.

As he sat down the young man shuffled the deck of cards repeatedly. His wristbands and bracelets rattled against the table. He then heard Denise's footsteps walk down the aisle; she placed another drink down on the table, looked at him and smiled.

"The captain said we're taking off shortly. Hopefully we will beat the oncoming storm. Sorry for the delay."

"Can you see this man? He is the reason the take-off is delayed."

"Are you feeling, okay? I only see you!"

He scanned the cabin frantically, but the young man had disappeared.

"I'm fine." Louie said, trying to recompose himself beneath Denise's quizzical gaze.

He sat speechless as he tried to figure out if Denise had apart to play in this charade. As she disappeared, Louie shook his head in frustration. The strange young man reappeared and started to split the deck of cards; he again shuffled each split without looking. Then he waved his hand over the cards, and they disappeared.

The plane began to taxi down the runway, so he buckled himself in, but he did not take his eyes off the

A Small Book

young man. He looked through the window when lightning struck the ground in the distance. Instantly his eyes returned to the young man who had not moved. His blue eyes were transfixed on Louie, as they ascended. Finally, the plane levelled off and began to cruise.

"Don't you just hate awkward silences." The young man suddenly said, looking at Louie. "Deeney is my name and magic is my game."

"Really?"

"Is that too much? A little overkill?"

"Guessing you have been rehearsing that one for some time? I'm afraid I've seen your parlour tricks before." Louie said, derisively.

"All I ask is for a chance, a chance to convince you. Then maybe we can work on the deal that will make you richer than you already are."

"Convince me! I've seen many so-called magicians over the years. What makes you any different?"

"Well, let me show you what I'm capable of."

"Well, it's not like you can leave, is it? You may as well try to entertain me until we land." Louie said with a dismissive wave of his hand.

"No problem."

"So, do you have a first name?"

"Yes, but everyone calls me Deeney."

With his drink in hand he sat back in his chair and signalled Deeney, the imaginary stage is his. The young man bowed his head gratefully. With a flick of his wrist a deck of cards appeared, and he placed them on the table.

"Please open the deck. As you can see, they are new and unopened."

As he held the deck in his hand, Louie read the name Jillette, which seemed familiar. He peeled off the plastic wrapping and slid the cards out. As he placed them on the table Deeney fanned them out.

"Pick a card. Any card, don't let me see it, though."

An impatient sigh left Louie's lips. He placed his finger on one card and slid it across the table. He peeked at the card; the six of hearts. Deeney placed the cards in a pile.

"Please, cut the deck?"

He split the deck into two equal piles, Deeney then picked up the cards and shuffled them six times.

"Please, cut the deck again?"

He repeated the instructions and witnessed Deeney shuffle them again a further three times.

"Is this where you ask me to pick a number between one and whatever? Then you start to remove each pile one by one, until you have one pile left and then you do the same to that pile until we have my

A Small Book

card left. Please don't, I've seen this a thousand times before."

"Now please could you cut the deck into six piles?"

Begrudgingly Louie cut the deck again, his patience had now disappeared.

"OK, ok." Deeney said, holding his hands out to placate the older, irate man.

Surprised at how calm Deeney seemed to be, even with his outburst. But then shocked as he watched each pile disappear right before his eyes. Then Deeney fanned out the last pile one card the six of hearts faced upward as the others faced down. Slowly, Deeney moved the card across the table.

"Take the card as you will need it later."

"Why should I bother?" As he looked down at it.

"Trust me, Mr. Howell, you will need this."

As he picked the card up, he flexed it and checked the corners. It had to be a rigged card; but as he flipped it over it became completely blank on both sides.

"Seeing as you didn't think much of the card trick, let's see what you think of this one" The young man said.

As he took another sip of his drink, he watched Deeney begin to meditate and mutter something under his breath. After, another sip Louie choked as he watched blue sparks travel over Deeney's hands. As he separated them the sparks jumped from hand to hand. Intently Louie looked for wires. But he caught the face of Deeney whose eyes focused on the lightshow. Sparks leapt about obediently in arcs between his hands. Then they disappeared.

"OK, could be deemed impressive," Louie said, trying to regain his composure. "Have you rigged something in your wristbands?"

"Still not convinced, are we?" The young man looked up at Louie with a grin.

"Guessing you won't quit, will you?"

"Well Mr. Howell. Convincing you means I can convince the world. You can create the platform for me to work my...magic!"

"I can create a platform for you?"

"Yes, you can, a grand stage, which magic deserves."

"You have only shown me carefully planned parlour tricks."

"Parlour tricks, Mr. Howell you're wrong. I am not a fake magician, who uses sleight of hand and misdirection."

"You're telling me you're a real magician?" Louie said cynically.

"When you open your eyes to it, you will see."

Confidently, Deeney strolled towards a set of cupboards. He slid the latch open which revealed a

A Small Book

worktop and a drawer which he pulled open. As he glanced at Louie, he pulled out a knife, which he started to spin around in his hand.

"What are you doing?" Louie said, tensing in his seat.

"Relax, Mr. Howell, this isn't for you, it's for my next trick."

"Well, that's good to know," Louie took another sip of his drink before edging further into his chair as Deeney came back to the table.

He watched Deeney as he moved the knife over his left arm, searching for the perfect spot. A strange symbol which looked like red brush strokes is where he stopped. One straight line the other a curved line crossed through it: underneath were two red circles. He pierced his flesh with the blade and drew it down his arm. Blood dripped from the wound onto the table, but it never fell off the table, as if some invisible barrier stopped it. Amazed and horrified by what he had watched, Louie couldn't believe how Deeney seemed unfazed and calm.

"Now, Mr. Howell, think of something you hold very dear, something you have never told anyone?"

"You're deranged, to cut yourself open like you did! "

"I need you to see what I am capable of. Have you thought of what you hold dear."

129

A D Small

"I have it."

"Good. Now let's begin."

He watched as Deeney placed both hands over the small puddle of blood. Again he muttered some words, and the crimson pool began to ripple. The young man moved his hands to the left, and it followed, then right and it followed again. As he raised his hands, the blood formed a cylindrical tower. The blood still rippled like a lava lamp which mesmerized Louie.

"You underestimate me." The young man said, looking deep into Louie's eyes. "Now I need you to visualize the thing you hold dear. "

As Deeney moved his hands, the blood slowly formed a set of numbers.

"27.06.2007, clearly an important date for you."

"No way, impossible."

"Now do you, see? "

More words were muttered by Deeney as he placed his hand over the open wound. When he removed his hand, Louie's jaw dropped as the wound had disappeared. The tattoo untouched, no damaged skin, even the blood had vanished.

"Well, Mr. Deeney, this wasn't my plan for this evening. So, what else have you got? Impress me! "

Disturbed by the sights he had seen; Louie collapsed into his chair and took the last gulp from his glass. The meeting with two executives regarding a

130

A Small Book

potential new entertainment show; could be the next big thing, he wanted to be able to deliver a great pitch for it. But the appearance of Deeney threw all those plans into disarray. His mind raced with many questions? But on the outside, he held a straight face.

"Oh, I will impress you, before the night is over" The young man said with a playful, wicked grin.

As Deeney stood and turned around, Louie's heart started to race as he saw Deeney's eyes turn bright blue. He wondered what would happen next. This reminded him of a film called, Demon Plane. The film did not end well for the main character, but he tried to force the horrific images of the contorted bodies and faces from his mind.

He sank deeper into his chair when Deeney began to shake violently, he heard the bones pop and crack. Then the young man opened his mouth and screamed silently. A blue glow came from Deeney's throat, as it moved into his mouth it turned into electricity. Sparks jumped from his mouth and shot around the plane as he turned his head right then left before he looked back at Louie. He then shook violently one more time before electricity shot from his hands and into the electrical sockets of the plane.

. . .

A D Small

His mind raced, but he could not look away. He wanted to figure out how he did the trick. The plane shook briefly then stopped, and the final bits of electricity left Deeney who then collapsed to his knees. How had he managed it Louie thought? The relative silence of the cabin returned, and Louie looked around, expecting the crew to come forth. But it didn't happen, Louie allowed himself a cynical smile.

"So, you somehow managed to set this charade up with the pilot and the crew? I see the stewardess has not been in to check on us both. Hidden cameras and smoke machines..., mirrors, no doubt."

"A non-believer, still, are we?" The young man said, looking up at Louie.

"Am I truly, supposed to believe what you've shown me is actual magic?"

"In time you will."

"In time? You're sadly mistaken. I am not easily fooled."

"Mr. Howell, you will soon open your eyes to what I have shown you."

"You keep telling me that."

"When you believe, I will find you."

"That will be never then."

After he regained his strength, Deeney grabbed his coat from the chair. As he put it on, he reached inside the pocket, and removed a deck of cards. With the

132

A Small Book

cards in his hand he began to split the deck and shuffle them without taking his eyes off Louie.

"Well, Mr. Howell, thank you for your patience, but it is time I... disappeared." said with a wry smile.

"We're in mid-flight, you can't exactly walk out the door!"

No response came, instead Deeney began to recite a mantra. He started to move the cards around, splitting the deck and shuffling them in each hand. The words spoken were unrecognisable. In one swift hand movement, Deeney threw them towards the mirror. None of the cards hit the floor they just floated in mid-air and began to move around as if caught in a small storm. As seconds passed, the cards moved around faster and faster. With a wink, Deeney stepped into the cyclone of cards and disappeared. The cards continued their manic, cyclic dance before the wind ushered them towards the mirror and

they disappeared.

The closer Louie stepped towards the mirror he saw something stuck to it. His eyes widened when he saw the six of hearts. He placed his hand on the mirror and tried to peel it free. But the card now sat on the inside of the mirror. He ran his hand around the mirror and over the cabin wall; there had to be a hidden panel and a compartment, but nothing. His head spun around to the toilet at the back of the cabin. No red

A D Small

light, nowhere else Deeney could be. A shift in attitude fell across Louie, could magic be real he thought. His brain fought against what it saw and logic. He sat back down, confused, conflicted with his eyes focused on the mirror. Graceful steps echoed around his head, but his gaze never wavered.

"Are you okay? Mr. Howell?"

"Yeah...yeah ...I'm fine," Louie said, trying to recompose himself.

"Please, buckle yourself in? We're making our descent shortly."

"Yeah ... sure...sure. "

"This turbulence will pass, "Denise said with a reassuring smile. "Mr. Howell. Captain Teller is a great pilot."

As Denise left the cabin, Louie fastened his seat belt, but he still couldn't take his eyes off the mirror. How did the cards disappear and yet one card managed to stick to the inside of the mirror? The questions filled his mind as he searched for the logic. Again Louie's eyes drifted towards the toilet. Then the plane began to shake.

"I am sure he is, but he can't control the weather, can he? "

The plane started to descend, and he could see the

A Small Book

lights from the runway of Anderson Airport. As Louie looked out of the window; his hands gripped the arms of the chair as the plane fought against the weather. His eyes refocused on the mirror and the card to take his mind off the turbulence.

Once the plane broke through the storm it deployed its landing gears and slowly touched down on the brightly lit runway. He unclipped his buckle and headed for the door, he had to get off and look.

"Mr. Howell, please return to your seat!" Denise said from behind him.

The words were heard but the desire to check the outside of the plane had a greater pull. He brushed Denise's hand away. If he could see Deeney climb out of a secret compartment of the undercarriage. It would give him the answer he needed and explain the events he had witnessed on this flight.

"Mr. Howell, please stop!"

"I have to see, quickly open this blasted door. "

"Mr. Howell, what are you talking about?"

"You have to be in on this!" Louie said, turning back to look into her shocked eyes, "You all have to be. I need to see."

He pushed passed Denise as she opened the door, without thinking he moved down the steps two at a time. As he landed on the floor, he looked under the plane. His eyes scanned every panel as he searched for

A D Small

the secret door, but with the only light source coming from the runway, he saw nothing. As the rain poured, he stood there and just stared at the plane. He willed Deeney to make an appearance and ignored the crew around him. When the rain stopped hitting him, he snapped back to reality.

"There you go, Mr. Howell."

"Oh, Austin. "

"Come on, Sir. Let's get you out of the rain. "

"He has to appear."

"Who, Sir?"

"Deeney."

"I watched you land, and I didn't see anyone jump from the plane."

"Are you sure?"

"Positive sir; I would stake my job on it. Let's get you in the car."

The words cut through Louie's paranoia, but what had happened on the plane could not have been his imagination. He also knew Austin would not lie. The entire impromptu audition played through his mind as Louie climbed into the limousine. He sat there trying to find the logic in the chaos. He watched Austin as he sat in the driver's seat and started the engine. They pulled away from the airstrip. As they passed all the hangers towards the security gate, Louie looked through the tinted glass praying to see Deeney so he

136

A Small Book

could validate what he had witnessed. He couldn't shake the notion the hostess and pilots were in on it, they had to be. Magic over the years had been labelled as misdirection and sleight of hand; not real. He reached into his pocket and removed the card Deeney had given him. As he flipped it around in his hand both sides were still completely blank. The car pulled up to the security gates; Austin lowered the window and showed his pass, then the gates opened.

As they moved through the city, Louie opened the window to get some air to try and relax. The sound of the traffic, music from bars, and the smells of freshly cooked food filled the limousine. He slowly inhaled and exhaled; his heart slowed. The car passed through a pair of large, black metal gates to his home. He just wanted to climb into his bed and forget the whole night if he could. The limousine parked next to a set of steps which led to a large oak door. As Austin followed Louie up to the mansion.

"Are you going to be okay, Mr. Howell?"

"Thank you, Austin, I will be fine. It has been a long week."

"I can only imagine. If there's nothing else you need, I'll wish you good night, sir."

"Same to you, Austin."

The front door opened, and old gentleman welcomed Louie.

"Evening, sir. "

"Evening, Joseph."

He looked across the garden and pondered the day's events, angry about the auditions and the curiosity of the weird flight home. The whole crew had to be in on the prank from Deeney.

Pleasantries and the suitcase were exchanged between Austin and Joseph which snapped Louie from his thoughts. But why would they want to orchestrate the prank, what would the endgame be.

"I have placed your suitcase in your master bedroom."

As the door closed behind him, Louie looked into the hall of his home. Joseph walked down the stairs.

"Thank you, Joseph, please could you fetch me a pot of tea, I will be in my study."

"Of course, Sir."

Slowly Louie walked down the hall, left of the staircase. He stepped through a door which led to a square room. All the walls were an off-white except the light grey feature wall. A large thick glass desk sat near the back wall. As he collapsed into his chair, he turned on his computer. The aroma of peppermint filled Louie's nostrils before Joseph entered the room. He placed a tray next to the computer monitor and poured out a cup of tea, before dropping in a sugar cube.

A Small Book

"Would you like milk sir?"

"No thank you."

"Will you need anything else sir?"

"That will be all for tonight."

As he bid Joseph good night, he pulled the card from his pocket and placed it on the table. He examined it and then flipped the card around a few times. Nothing, still completely blank. With the meeting less than 24 hours away he opened the document on his computer, 'A new talent show', he had created it but needed to acquire a channel to show it. The first refusal fell to the current network executives Raymond Blaine and Charles Copperfield. Even with the popularity of his current show he needed the executives to sign off on it. His money had been made in his record label. But he had acquired a number of artists from the show, but any more shows needed to be authorised. He read through the pitch and then started to alter it. The words 'show name' were still blank, undecided on the names he had come up with. He checked the note pad on his desk, it read British Bandstand, Bands Got Talent and Becoming A Star. As he spun a pen around his fingers, his phone rang, screen read Sandy Cahill, his personal assistant, as he answered he activated the speaker and left the phone on the desk.

"Hello, Mr. Howell."

"Yes, Sandy. "

"I know it is late, but I had to call regarding the meeting tomorrow."

"Are they rescheduling?"

"Unfortunately, sir, the network PR team have informed me. Mr. Copperfield and Mr. Blaine both passed away early this evening."

"Is this a joke?"

"It's not, sir. I have checked the news sites, and I can confirm it is true."

"That is incredibly sad news. Please, can you arrange for some flowers to be delivered? "

"I have already ordered them, sir."

"Thank you, Sandy. Please, could you send me the links to the news sites."

A ping sound came from his computer, then the notification off Sandy appeared in the bottom corner. He clicked on the link and sipped his cup of tea, as the page loaded.

"I will keep you informed of the rescheduling of the meeting. "

"Thank you. I will see you in the office tomorrow. "

"OK, Sir."

Shocked by the terrible news he remembered the few times he had encountered Mr Blaine and Mr Copperfield. They were always friendly and honest men, with young families. The nation named Louie

A Small Book

Mr Nasty, but he did have a heart and it went out to the families who lost the two men. As his eyes read through the article, the contents of his stomach slowly crawled up his throat. The journalist named Daniel McGee stated the police had commented 'no foul play had been involved', just two men had died through freak accidents. Police had confirmed Mr. Charles Copperfield had been found in the gardens of 6 Penn Square at approximately 20:07. Cause of death, being impaled on a malfunctioned water sprinkler, which filled his lungs up with water.

The horrific news terrified Louie. As he worked his way through the article, it stated Mr Raymond Blaine had died in a night club, some faulty wiring had caused his cardiac arrest. A witness said his screams echoed around the club and the smell of burnt flesh will haunt them forever. An image of the club came across the screen, Louie froze in horror. On the screen sat the numbers 6, 20:07 and 27 as he re-arranged them in his mind, he reached into his pocket and removed the card. As he spun the card around the words, Hugh Deeney, real magician, appeared. Then from the couch opposite the desk came a voice, which caused his heart to race.

"Don't you just hate awkward silences!"

141

Acknowledgments

Just want to thank the people below for all their help and support in creating this book, that you have read.

- *Denise Knott*
- *Dan Barnes*
- *Paul C England*
- *John Bentley*
- *Dave Horsley*
- *Jesse D'Angelo*
- *Sam Walker*
- *Stephen Kempt*
- *John Isles*
- *Letty Seddon*
- *Scott Pratt*
- *Stephen Coyle*
- *Dan Stratford*
- *J.L, Heath*
- *Dihn Bailey*
- *Ashes Wainwright*
- *Christian Francis*

Paul C England kindly edited a number of the stories in this book. An excellent editor, who I highly recommend, he is also an amazing writer in his own right. Currently he is finalising the last edit of *The Line: Dog Eat Dog*.

About A D Small

Picture by bentleyportraits.co.uk

I have had a passion for writing for twenty-six years now. In that time I have written a number of stories varying in length; but since joining a local writer's group, I have developed a love for writing poetry. Since my last book 'A Mind Full of Words', I have been working on and putting together a collection of short stories for you to read. This will hopefully be the one of many. Look out for further publications.

To my readers, I thank you for taking the time to read my work and hope you enjoy them as much as I did creating them.

My plans are to release more short stories and novels over the coming months/years as well as more poems. I love creating and I hope you continue to follow me through my journey.

linktr.ee/adsmallauthor

- facebook.com/adsmallauthor
- x.com/ADSmallauthor
- instagram.com/adsmallauthor
- tiktok.com/@adsmallauthor
- linkedin.com/in/a-d-small-6b2653192

Books By A D Small

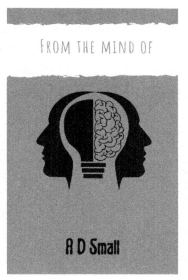 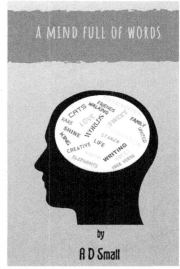

From The Mind Of and *A Mind Full of Words* are anthologies of poetry, I have written about my experiences, fears, and triumphs. I wrote about real-life love, loss, and grief. With the extra time to reflect this year, the collection has poems about the past, present and my hopes for the future.

Printed in Great Britain
by Amazon